SUPREME

&

JUSTICE 3

ERNEST MORRIS

Good2Go Publishing

SUPREME & JUSTICE 3

Written by Ernest Morris
Cover Design: Davida Baldwin
Typesetter: Mychea
ISBN: 9781947340077
Copyright ©2017 Good2Go Publishing
Published 2017 by Good2Go Publishing
7311 W. Glass Lane • Laveen, AZ 85339
www.good2gopublishing.com
https://twitter.com/good2gobooks
G2G@good2gopublishing.com
www.facebook.com/good2gopublishing
www.instagram.com/good2gopublishing

ACKNOWLEDGMENTS

First and foremost, I have to thank God once again for keeping me focused long enough to produce another novel.

Second, I would like to thank all my readers for supporting me and keeping me motivated to bring you into my world whether it be fiction or nonfiction.

A special shout-out goes to my homie EDWARD MOSES. Keep your head up, and be safe. Time heals all wounds, bro, and you're a fighter. Trust me, I know!

Shout out to my brothers: Kevin (Chubb) and Sedric (Walid) Morris. Rasheed, Frank, and Maurice Turner.

Thanks to Googd2Go Publishing for continuing to believe in me.

Shout out to Leneek, Nakisha, Brandi, Kendra, Meana, Le'Shea, Shayana, Sahmeer, Demina, Bo, Dee, Tysheeka, Tasha, Barry, Richard (RIP), Aliyah aka Fish (RIP), Queanna, Dwunna Theresa, Loveana, Ty, Peanut, Janell, Trina, Markida, Sharon, Aneatra, Phyllis, Eric, Andre, Eddie, Tamara, Janay,

Bey, Yahnise, Nyia, Pamela, Symiya, Mira, Alisha, Shannon, Dee Dee, Damien, Nafeese, Kenya, Nyeemah, My Cheesecake Family, etc. Anyone else that I forgot to mention, it wasn't intentional, but thank you also. I've done it again!!!!

PROLOGUE

Justice drove down the street in his new Cadillac truck. After getting out of a bad situation, he wanted to play it cool for a while. The streets were praising him and his brother for the magic trick they had performed. They really had the keys to the city now. Their plug handed over literally sixty keys of heroin for free, thanks to Chris saving his sister's life.

Justice wanted his brother to fall back from the operation and hopefully get the degree they had talked about, but Supreme loved what they had going right now. Justice believed this was the chance for Supreme to enroll in law school. He knew he would object to it, so he took the liberty of contacting Supreme's old therapist, Karen, and together they were able to pull a few strings to make it happen. Now Justice had to deliver the good news.

"Yo, Bro, where are you right now?" Justice asked once Supreme answered.

"I'm just now getting off of I-95. What's up?"

"I need to talk to you," Justice said.

"I'll be there soon as I drop this money off to Chris. He was supposed to pick that shit up, but he's caught up with some bitch again. We need to have a talk with him when we see him. MOB, Bro, you know how we do," Supreme replied.

"Say no more! Anyway, make sure you stop past. I have some important news for you."

"No doubt," Supreme told him, ending the call.

Twenty minutes later, Supreme was driving down 5th and Cambria to meet up with Chris. Just as he was cruising through the stop sign, he heard sirens coming from behind him. When he looked in his rearview mirror, he saw the flashing lights.

"Fuck!" he said, pulling over.

Supreme eased his .40 cal. from his waist and slid

it inside the glove compartment. He quickly locked it before the officer exited the car. Then he rolled the window down, hoping to get rid of the loud smell, before he reached in the side panel for his paperwork.

"What did I do officer? I wasn't speeding or anything, so why am I being pulled over?" Supreme asked, staring up at the plain-clothes officers.

"You want to know what you did, huh?" the officer with the tie replied. "You and your bitch-ass lawyer tried to manipulate the system, but you're not above the law. Step out of the car, now!"

Supreme stepped out of the car and was pushed up against the hood. They searched him for anything illegal, but he was clean. They never searched his car, which told him they were just trying to harass him.

"Listen, I don't know what you're talking about," Supreme said. He knew they thought he was Justice, so he played along so they wouldn't find out.

"We will be keeping our eyes on you. You will

slip up, and when you do, we'll be there to watch you fall for good. Enjoy the rest of your day," the other officer stated, letting him go.

The cops hopped in their unmarked car, then sped off. Supreme waited until they turned the corner, before getting back into his car. He sat there emptying the contents of the Dutch out, then filling it with loud. Just as he was about to spark it, someone tapped on the window. Supreme looked up to see a gun aimed directly at his head. He never had the chance to do anything as the gunman fired a barrage of bullets into the car, hitting him with all seventeen shots.

The gunman then jumped into the approaching car and fled the scene. Supreme tried to move but couldn't. Through his heavy breathing, all he could think about was his brother and the little bit of time they had shared together. He wished he would have had the chance to talk to him one more time, but he didn't. That was the last thing he remembered before taking his last breath and falling into eternal darkness.

~ ~ ~

"It's done! Now you have to keep your end of the deal," the caller said.

"Don't tell me what I have to do, got it?"

"I was just saying," the caller began, but was cut off.

"You wasn't saying anything. You were just listening. I want my streets back by any means, and you're gonna help me get them. Are we clear?"

"Crystal!" the caller responded.

And now the sequel to *SUPREME & JUSTICE I & II*. . .

ONE

"Oh damn, that's right! Suck it, baby," Justice moaned as the neighborhood slut gave him some head inside his SUV.

The windows were tinted so no one could see inside. Wannie had the best head in Philly, and here he was finding out firsthand. She continued until his balls finally tensed up and he exploded in her mouth. She swallowed every ounce of cum, not missing a single drop. Justice was damn near climbing the back of the seat, trying to get away.

"I told you ain't no bitch out here fucking with me," she said, wiping her mouth.

"I want some of that pussy now."

"You got a condom?"

"No! Shit, you just swallowed all that nut. I'm not going to bust inside you," he said, feeling inside her jeans. "I'll pull out as soon as I feel myself about to bust."

He started playing with her pussy, causing her to instantly moisten up. Wannie closed her eyes, then spread her legs to give him some extra room to work. Justice took that as the opportunity to go further, and started sliding her jeans off. Once they were off, he found himself staring at the fattest pussy he had ever seen. It was cleanly shaved, and her clit poked out as if it was waiting to be fondled.

"Shhiittt," Wannie moaned when his finger started flicking her clit. It felt so good that she almost didn't notice Justice trying to slide up in her raw. "Wait, wait! I said you need a condom. No glove, no love, nigga."

"Stop being a tease. You know you want some of this," he replied, taking her hand and wrapping it around his shaft.

The feeling alone almost made her cum. She

started stroking his dick, feeling his veins pulsating under the skin. Wannie really wanted to fuck his rich ass, but she wasn't trying to catch another STD. She kissed the tip of his dick, then looked him in the eyes.

"Let's go to the store and grab a condom real quick. I guarantee you, it will be worth the wait."

"Well since you put it that way, let's go," he said, rolling the passenger side window down. He yelled something to his workers, then pulled off.

He drove around to 37th and Fairmont and parked in front of the bodega. Wannie threw on her jeans, hopped out of the SUV, and went inside to grab what she needed. When she came back out and got back in the car, Justice was smoking some loud.

"Can I have a hit?" Wannie asked.

"Sure, while I'm hitting that," Justice replied reaching between her thighs.

"Go to my crib. We can chill there."

He pulled up in front of Wannie's house and

parked. When they stepped out of the vehicle, she placed her hand on his erection and led him inside. They walked into the living room, and she sat on the couch without taking her hand from his penis. While one hand massaged his dick, the other was tugging at the sweatpants he was wearing, pulling them down to his ankles.

Justice stood there with his erection standing proudly as she stroked it until it was at full strength once again. Wannie stood up, then pushed him down on the couch. Justice watched her as she slowly and sexually removed her jeans and shirt. She only had her panties left, and she was kind enough to bend over, giving him a full view of her goodies as she slid them off. She sat down next to Justice, trying to kiss him on the mouth. He turned his head.

"I don't kiss," he stated firmly. "If we fucking, let's get it. Other than that, I have shit to do."

"Whatever," she replied as if she had an attitude.

She ripped the condom open and slid it down his dick. Justice positioned himself to enter her hot box. Her breathing quickened as he knelt above her, spreading her legs. He eased his body between them and guided his throbbing cock into her hole. Wannie's pussy was so warm, moist, and tight that being inside it was an indescribable pleasure. She met each thrust with one of her own, and he could feel his balls quickly tensing again.

"Fuck, I'm about to cum."

"No, not yet," Wannie panted. Her body started moving faster, trying to catch up to him hoping they came together.

"Too late!" he said, releasing his semen into the condom.

Wannie was a bit frustrated that she didn't get hers. She watched Justice fix his clothes back and head toward the door.

"So that's it?" she asked.

"I have to go meet up with my brother. Right now that's more important than anything. I haven't heard anything from him, and there's money to be made. This is for you though," he said, peeling off a couple of twenties and passing them to her.

Once he left, she lifted her legs in the air, then placed two fingers into her pussy. It didn't take her long to get what she needed as her juices squirted all over her fingers.

~ ~ ~

BEEP! BEEP! BEEP! BEEP!

The sound of the respirator was the only reason the man lying there was breathing. It'd been two days since he had gone in a coma, with no signs of improvement. The nurse came in to give him a quick sponge bath, when a detective walked up on her.

"Do you have any idea when he will wake up?"

"You will have to speak to the doctor about that. If you will wait here, I'll go see if I can find him for you," she replied, leaving the room.

As soon as the detective made sure the nurse was out of sight, he walked over and stood by the patient's bedside. He looked at the monitor, then at the sleeping patient.

"Motherfucker, would you just die, for crying out loud," he whispered. "You're a fucking piece of shit, and you're lucky I don't put a slug through your skull right now. Matter of fact, you don't deserve to be breathing on this either."

The detective squeezed on the tube that ran from the machine to his mouth. It stopped the air circulation he was receiving, causing the patient to lose air. His breathing suddenly stopped, causing the alarm on the monitor to go off.

BEEEEEEEEEEEEEP!

The detective immediately released the hose when he heard all the footsteps rushing toward the room. He backed up just as they entered with the crash cart.

"Detective, I'm gonna have to ask you to leave now so that we can work on the patient," the doctor said as his team went to work.

"I'll be right outside the door. We need him alive," the detective replied.

Once he walked out of the room, he headed over to the nurses' station to chat with the charge nurse. She was busy typing on the computer when he walked up. She looked up with a smile on her face.

"Can I help you, Officer?"

"Yes, you can, ma'am. Have any family members come to see the patient that's in room 206 yet?"

"Let me check for you," she said, hitting a couple keys, then shaking her head. "Not as of this morning. The only one that has been here is you, and the officers that came in with him and the paramedics."

"Thank you!"

He waited a few more minutes until the doctor walked out removing his hat. The look on his and the nurse's faces said it all. He gave the detective a look as if the patient didn't make it, then walked into the next room to check on his other patients. The detective walked out of the hospital with a smile on his face.

~ ~ ~

"Why the fuck don't nobody know where my brother is?" Justice snapped.

He was standing in one of his trap houses with eight of his workers. It had been two days since the last time he talked to Supreme, and he was worried. If anything happened to his brother, he was going to shut the city down in blood. Every person in the trap house was on the phone calling around trying to locate Supreme.

"Just," Leneek yelled, running into the crib out of breath. "I think I know where Preme is."

"Neek, what the fuck you talking about?" he asked anxiously. He had lost him once, and he wasn't trying to lose him again.

"My friend said there was a shooting down her way the other day, but she never thought nothing of it until I called her. She said she seen Preme's car being towed away when her and her mom was turning on the block."

"Where was that?" Justice asked with rage.

As soon as she told him, he ran out the door with all his crew right behind him. He knew if Supreme was hurt, he would be at University Hospital. They all piled into two different vehicles and rushed toward the expressway. No words were spoken as everyone was in deep thought, hoping Preme was okay. When they pulled up in front of the hospital, Justice and Leneek ran into the hospital. Justice walked up to the reception desk and asked about Supreme. The nurse checked for his brother's name.

"He looks just like me," Justice said, knowing that Preme probably didn't have his ID on him. "He is my twin brother."

One of the doctors on duty recognized Justice and stopped in her tracks. She thought she was seeing things until she heard him say "twin." She rushed over and pulled Justice to the side.

"Listen, we've been trying to find out who he was but couldn't. Your brother is in an induced coma. He shouldn't even be alive after taking seventeen shots to his upper body. He is a very lucky man," the doctor told him.

"I want to see him," Supreme demanded. "Take me to my brother."

"Follow me!"

The doctor led Justice to his brother's room. As soon as he saw him, he wanted to snap the fuck out. Supreme lay peacefully, sleeping like a baby. Leneek stayed near the door, scared to see him lying there like that. His whole body was bandaged up.

"Who did this to you, Bro?" Justice asked, holding his brother's hand.

Tears were forming in his eyes, but he refused to let one drop. It was now time to lay something down, and anyone he had beef with was on his hit list. If he only knew who was really behind this mess, it would have saved a lot of blood that was about to be shed.

TWO

Chris was driving through traffic recklessly, trying to get over to the hospital where Supreme was being held. He had received a phone call from Leneek that Justice wanted bloodshed in the streets until somebody came forward with information about his brother. Instead of carrying out his orders, he wanted to make sure Justice was good first.

As soon as he exited the expressway, he noticed a familiar car cruising past him at a moderate speed. Chris quickly retrieved his gun from under the seat and clicked the safety off. His whole demeanor changed when the car pulled into the gas station, then parked next to an unmarked police car.

"Fucking snitch, I'm gonna bury you," he mumbled to himself. "Another place, and another time, you bitch-ass nigga."

BOOM! BOOM! BOOM!

Chris ducked just in time as his passenger side window shattered. He threw his car in reverse and hit the gas in an effort to get away.

BOOM! BOOM! BOOM!

Three more shots shattered the front window. Glass shards hit Chris in the face causing him to almost lose control of his vehicle. His driving skills were on point, and he was able to regain control before hitting a parked pickup truck. Chris raised his Desert Eagle and let off six rounds, trying to give himself some distance to get the hell out of there.

The two cars both swerved, avoiding a head-on collision with a Brinks truck. That was the opening Chris needed. He gassed the Dodge Magnum, and the engine roared through the red light, heading down Grays Ferry. He checked in his rearview and didn't see anyone following him. After driving over the bridge, he pulled over on a side street to wipe the blood from his face. Something wasn't right about the situation he had just seen. He wondered why a cop would be taking shots at him in broad daylight. He needed to let Justice know what was going on, and fast. Shit just hit the fan!

"Answer your phone," Chris whispered, listening to Justice's phone ringing. Once the voicemail came on, he left a message, then ended the call. He turned around and headed for the hospital. He needed to let his brother know what was going on.

~ ~ ~

Elizabeth drove her Toyota Camry through the section of Philly called the Badlands, trying to hurry up and drop the work off so she could head back to Delaware. Ever since the day Supreme and Justice linked back up, they had the city on smash. Supreme made Elizabeth in charge of a few spots to get her off his back. She knew her brother was destined to be something special, but never did she think he would have blown up like that. She regretted that she didn't give him some pussy when he tried that night. Maybe she could have been his bitch. To her it wasn't incest because they weren't blood related.

This neighborhood was one of the roughest areas of Philadelphia. People were bound to die at any given time from a bullet, knife, dope, etc. Nothing was off limits in the Badlands. Elizabeth wasn't afraid though because her brother ran the area, so people respected anyone that was linked to him. She still always watched her surroundings whenever she came through, just like Supreme had taught her.

Maybe her train of thought was making her paranoid, but when she stopped the car at a stop sign, she immediately noticed the young Hispanic male walking across the street. He purposely took his time when he got in front of Elizabeth's car as if he was trying to hold her up. Her instincts told her something wasn't right about this guy. Upon further inspection, she noticed that his attire also screamed a warning. He was dressed in all black from head to toe: big black hoodie, baggy black jeans, and black Timberland boots. Elizabeth didn't want to stereotype him, because, after all, she was in the hood delivering dope to workers.

Suddenly, in one swift motion, the man stopped directly in front of her car, pulled out a large gun from beneath his hoodie, and pointed the barrel directly at Elizabeth's head. He moved from the front of the car to the back passenger side, keeping the weapon trained on her the whole time. Her eyes darted around the area as the surreal event unfolded. Her mind raced with thoughts of escape, yet her driving foot didn't move an inch off the brake pedal.

"Bitch, pull off and I'll kill you!" he said as if he could read her mind.

The man put enough emphasis behind his words

that Elizabeth believed him. She wasn't willing to gamble with her life. He appeared jumpy and volatile, and she knew one wrong move could set him off. The gunman proceeded to the passenger's door. He pulled the handle, but the car door didn't open. It was locked.

"Bitch, open the fucking door! Now!" he shouted.

Elizabeth complied, opening the door with a touch of a button. She thought he was trying to carjack her, so she would give up the car as long as he didn't get the work. Luckily it was in the stash box that Supreme had installed when he first bought her the car.

"You can have the car, just don't hurt me," Elizabeth said as the man entered the vehicle.

"Shut the fuck up and drive," the gunman yelled, poking the gun hard in her ribcage.

While Elizabeth followed his orders, he scanned

the area making sure no one had seen what happened. Confident that no one had, he focused his attention back on his victim, who at this point was a nervous wreck.

"You can have anything you want. Take my purse and car. Here, you can even have my phone so I can't call the cops," she said, starting to feel desperate. "Just let me go."

"Bitch, I said shut the fuck up and drive," he snapped even more aggressively than before. She had no clue of what was going on inside his head at the moment. "I don't want your fucking car, or anything else. I want you!"

Elizabeth felt everything inside her body freeze. She realized she was about to be kidnapped, and her hands started to shake. It was all she could do to keep from driving the car into a pole, she was so nervous. She had only read about this type of shit or seen it in movies. Never did she ever think it would happen to her.

She wished she'd had put the .25 caliber handgun Preme had given her in her purse like she was supposed to when coming out there. At this moment she wished she even saw a cop riding past, so she could alert him or her to the situation. That didn't look like it would be happening, so she complied with the man's request, just hoping she would make it out of this situation alive.

~ ~ ~

Ten minutes later, Elizabeth's wild ride ended just a few blocks from where it all began. From that point on she was led by gunpoint through an alleyway, into a dark house. Once inside, she was tied up and blindfolded. Two more accomplices later joined her original abductor, bringing the total number of people in attendance to three.

"Go get rid of her car, and hurry back," the gunman told the two men, just in case it was equipped with a LoJack device.

For about an hour Elizabeth was left alone in a dark room while her abductors performed various activities crucial to the success of their plan. The situation was surreal to Elizabeth. In her first few hours of captivity, she spent most of her time blinking away tears and fighting a guilty feeling of not being prepared like she should have been. If she made it out of this, they would never catch her slipping again.

Elizabeth had no choice but to assume the worst. Of all the thoughts racing through her mind at this point, death was the most prominent.

THREE

*L*ena arrived at her friend's house right after she got off work. Since her apartment was being renovated, Toya let her stay with her. Lena had worked at a strip club for about six months and was already tired of the place. On her way to Toya's crib, she had been thinking about another way to get money, but it was going to take some persuasion to gather some people to partake in her plan. As they got ready for bed, Lena decided to pitch her idea to her friend. If her plan was going to succeed, then she was going to also need someone that had party promotion experience.

"I gotta idea that I wanna put you down with," Lena said.

"I'm listening," Toya replied.

"Okay, dig, right. I know you're good at

throwing parties, right?"

"Yeah, and?" Toya shot back.

"Well, I thought of a hot idea tonight while on my way here," she stated.

"What, you wanna start throwing parties or something?" Toya interrupted her once again.

"Can I talk? Damn!" a frustrated Lena asked.

"Go 'head, my bad, girl. Speak your piece," Toya responded.

"Anyway, like I was saying," Lena said with an attitude, "since you ain't got no patience, I'ma make a long story short. Yeah, I wanna be a promoter. I want to throw parties, but not like the ones you throw. I wanna throw sex parties, and not the kind where bitches be selling fucking dildos and shit either. At my parties bitches gonna be selling pussy, pussy, and more pussy."

Lena paused for a moment to see if her words had any effect on her friend. She could tell by the smirk on Toya's face that she had struck a chord with her. She was obviously interested, so Lena continued.

"Since you're already doing your thing on the party tip, I figured me and you can combine what we know and do this shit. I got bitches lined up and ready to do whatever. All I need to know is, are you with it or what?" Her look said it all!

Scratching her chin as if she were silently weighing her options, Toya looked slyly at Lena. She knew she could count her in even before she verbally agreed.

"Sounds like a plan to me!" Toya said enthusiastically.

"Alright, listen, this is how we gonna do this."

That night in Toya's crib, the two friends laid the foundation for their company, which would later be known as Unleashed Productions. Lena and Toya became the chief architects of this grand sex-for-sale scheme. The two friends spent hours in deep conversation. As they ironed out the wrinkles of the plan, going over the positives and negatives, Toya gained a newfound respect for Lena's mind. She learned that her friend had business acumen, and she saw a side of her that she hadn't seen since they met in middle school.

There wasn't any class or school that could prepare them for the journey they were about to embark on. Either they had it or they didn't. Either they would succeed, or they would fail. There was no in between. Besides a financial gain, there was a lot more at stake here, namely Lena's pride. She felt she was destined to succeed. Since her life had been a series of setbacks and failures in one way or another, she desperately needed to believe that this venture was going to be successful. Besides that, she had no backup plan. The way Lena saw it, if all went well this could just be her ticket out of the strip club forever.

Whether Toya knew it or not, an evolution was about to take place. She was about to witness Lena's transformation from stripper to shrewd businesswoman. Lena also wanted to include her other best friend, Kreasha. She knew she didn't need to do any of this because her boyfriend was a very wealthy kingpin, but maybe she still wanted her own money. Besides that, she still had to convince some of the girls at the club to join her, which wouldn't be hard considering they were all money hungry hoes, down for whatever when it came to that paper.

"We're gonna fuck the game up," Toya said as they both burst out laughing, thinking about all the money they were about to make.

~ ~ ~

During the next week, the girls started spreading the word about their new business. They even had fliers printed up to help promote the anything goes sexfest. The graphic artist did a wonderful job on the fliers. There were three extremely beautiful females, half naked, surrounded by a bunch of champagne, sports cars, etc.

While Lena took care of the underworld crowd, Toya went after the nine-to-five working-class guys. She cross-promoted their event at her Grown & Sexy affairs. She got tons of verbal commitments from her regular clientele. She promised them the party would be off the chain and they would get their money's worth. To her surprise, the upcoming event drew interest from all kinds of men and females, from corporate types and blue collars, to gangsters from every city.

What Toya and Lena didn't know was, it also attracted some unwanted guest that was about to have their city under siege and people gunning for their friends in more ways than one.

FOUR

"If you can't finish the job, I'll find somebody who can."

"I was interrupted, but I'll get it done."

"And when you do, I will make sure that you are significantly rewarded for completing the task. It needs to be done before we can move on with the final project."

"All you have to do is supply me with the tools I need, and it will be handled before you finish taking your shit."

It was as if there was a camera watching from somewhere in the room, because he was actually in the bathroom on the toilet. He looked around at first, but then realized he was just speaking rhetorically.

"Check your trunk before you leave your house. You'll find what you need to get this done; then you can be on your way."

"Good! My two associates should be here within the hour, then it's game time."

"Keep me informed, and I'll even throw in a bonus if you bring me his head on a silver platter. I expect results, not excuses. So don't call me with anymore, or you're the one that will be sorry," he said before ending the call.

He finished up in the bathroom then went back to his desk and pulled out one of his expensive Cuban cigars. He lit it and took a long drag, letting the sweet-smelling aroma entice his nostrils. A knock on the door disrupted his train of thought.

"Come in!"

"Sir, you have visitors in the conference room requesting your immediate presence," his young beautiful secretary announced.

"Tell them I'll be there when I finish my cigar."

"Um, sir, I don't think you want to keep these

people waiting," she replied with skepticism in her voice. "They didn't look too happy."

Reluctantly, he knew exactly who was waiting, and what they wanted. This was the conversation he really had been trying to avoid, but now it was inevitable. His superiors were here for answers he didn't have.

"Thanks, Amanda!" he said.

He put out the cigar, grabbed his jacket, then headed to the conference room. There were seven people sitting around the table waiting for him when he walked in. He didn't even bother to sit down.

"Let's get this over with. Do you want the long version or the short one?" he asked.

"What I want is, to know what's going on and why you can't handle this one simple problem. I have to hear from my workers that this little dip shit is still breathing. How is it that a man with as much persuasion as you have can't even eliminate one person? I really don't get it."

"What did you want me to do, run up in a crowded hospital, guns blazing? It's not that fucking simple. I was this close to taking care of him, before the alarm went off."

"I think you need to watch your tone of voice when talking to people that can easily have you picking up trash on the side of the road."

"Don't threaten me," he replied with an aggressive tone.

"Okay, gentlemen, calm down. We are on the same side here. The enemies are out there ruining my streets with heroin. You have guests waiting outside in a dark green Audi 8. I think you know who they are and what they came to do. You have the green light as long as you get the job done."

"What about the feds?"

"They won't be a problem," the mayor stated, twitching in her seat. "You have the backing of every

ERNEST MORRIS

agency on this. If you look around, I have some of the top officials sitting here with us. All their resources are at your disposal. I get my orgasms from results, and right now I'm being deprived." That made everyone who was staring in other directions turn to the mayor. She smiled because now she had everyone's attention. "It's now or never, people. Handle your business."

With that said, everybody at the table stood up to leave, except the mayor and deputy. Once the room was empty, he walked over and stood in front of her.

"Do you trust him, ma'am?" he asked, sitting on the edge of the desk.

"No! That's why once he takes care of our primary target, I want you to take care of him, and the two men he hired. He knows we can't have any witnesses. Can you handle that?"

"Consider it done!"

"I need you to take care of one other problem

before you go," she said, raising her skirt up to her thighs. "I need to release some stress before I pick my daughter up from the airport. You'll do just fine for now."

With that said, he got down on his knees and pulled her panties to the side. She scooted to the edge of her seat as he buried his face in her vagina. He ate her pussy until she came in his mouth like a fountain.

"Damn, just what I needed," she said, wiping herself with his shirt. She stood up, fixed her skirt, then walked out without saying another word.

~ ~ ~

"Y'all ready to handle this shit?"

"That's what we're here for, right, to put in work! Where is the nigga at?" one of the hired assassins asked, cocking his weapon.

"University Hospital. You know this may be a suicide mission, right?"

They didn't say anything, which told him they

understood the risk they were about to take.

"You will be a half million dollars richer if you succeed . . ."

"You mean *when*," the one in the passenger seat cut in.

"Right, *when* you succeed. I will wire the money directly to your account upon confirmation."

"All you need to do is take us to the spot and stay out of the way," the driver stated. "Watch how we get down!"

The ball was now in their court. He was about to see if the Organization's half million was money well spent or not. When they pulled up to the hospital, the driver, whose name was Javier, parked near the emergency entrance because if things went as expected, they would be making an emergency exit.

"Grab the toys out the trunk," he told his partner Raymond.

He hopped out and grabbed two fully loaded Sig

P-90s with silencers.

"If there's someone in there with him, you know what to do, right?"

"Don't tell me how to do my job. I've been doing this shit since I was nine years old. This is what I live for," Javier replied sarcastically.

"Okay, I'll be right here just in case you need me to cover for you."

Raymond threw on a bulletproof vest that was inside the trunk, then closed it. Looking around he could see that the hospital was extra busy today, but that wasn't going to deter them from what they came here to do.

"Let's do this, partner," Raymond said, passing Javier his weapon. They tucked them inside their shirts, then entered the hospital with one thing on their mind: murder!

FIVE

Justice, Kreasha, and Leneek sat in the room with Supreme, who still hadn't come out of his coma. He had two of his workers standing outside the door, strapped. Even though security was in place, Justice didn't trust them. Whoever had tried to kill his brother still didn't know he had a twin. Justice knew that hit was meant for him, that's why it hurt so bad. Kreasha talked to her friend Lena earlier and decided she wasn't interested in the business offer she proposed. Kreasha needed to be there for her man, and nothing would stop that from happening.

"I'm going to get something to drink from the vending machine," Justice said. "Anybody want something?"

"I'll take a juice," Leneek replied.

"Me too!" Kreasha told him.

Justice walked out of the room, past his two henchmen, then headed down the hall toward the vending machine area. All the machines on that floor weren't working, so he headed down to the lobby. As he was turning the corner, he noticed two men getting off the elevator. He didn't think too much of it, until they both looked at him as if they'd seen a ghost. That instantly threw up warning signs in his head.

When they looked at each other, then back at him, Justice knew shit was about to get ugly. The bulges coming from their shirts, only confirmed his suspicions. He quickly reached behind his back for his gun, but it was too late. The two killers had already drawn theirs and were aiming in his direction.

BLACCCC! BLACCC! BLACCC!

BLOCA! BLOCA! BLOCA! BLOCA!

Justice ducked behind a wall, just as a bullet skimmed his face. He quickly let off a few shots to

ERNEST MORRIS

buy himself some time. He realized they were there to finish the job on his brother, and that wasn't happening. He had the element of surprise because they still didn't know about him.

BOOM! BOOM! BOOM! The first two shots were off, but the next one wasn't.

Raymond was hit in his left shoulder, trying to get out of the way. That was the moment Justice needed to get a better angle on his target. He got low and fired two more shots, catching Raymond in the chest. Javier watched his partner go down and fired in the direction of the two men who were reaching for their weapons.

BLACCC! BLACCC! BLACCC! BLACCC! The shots took both of Justice's henchmen out. They never had a chance to get a shot off.

"What the hell was that?" Kreasha said, looking toward the door.

"Justice!" Leneek replied, jumping out of the

chair.

She reached into her purse and pulled out her 9mm, then ran out the door. People that were on the floor were ducking into rooms for cover. She spotted Justice taking fire, and ran in his direction to help.

BOC! BOC! BOC! BOC!

The two men didn't expect the ambush and were caught off guard. Realizing they were outnumbered, they headed for the staircase. Security came through the doors, weapons aimed and ready. Javier fired, hitting one of the guards in the face. The other three officers started firing in his direction. One of them saw Leneek with her gun in hand, and turned toward her. Justice peeped the blitz, and with no hesitation, sent a barrage of bullets in the guard's direction. Justice's shots were so accurate that the guard caught all six rounds. All hell had broken loose inside the hospital, and it was time to get the fuck out of there.

The call came over the radio, and the detective

jumped out of his vehicle to intervene. He was just about to run inside, when Javier emerged from the entrance, helping his injured friend outside.

"Raymond's been hit," he yelled.

"Come on, this place is about to be swarming with cops. Watch your faces; there're cameras all over the place," he stated, opening the backdoor. After helping Raymond in, they were able to flee the scene unnoticed.

~ ~ ~

"You okay?"

"Yeah, but we need to get out of here now," Leneek said as they ducked into a room.

"I'm not leaving my brother here, Neek. He's a target to those motherfuckers, and we still don't know who it is," Justice replied.

"Okay, let's get him out of here then, but we can't stay here any longer. Whatever you have in mind, we have to act fast. There is about to be a shitload of police and other agencies storming this place in a couple of minutes."

Justice stashed their weapons. Then they both changed into nurse uniforms. They hurried back to Supreme's room, where four armed men were waiting. Justice reached for his gun, but forgot that he had stashed it.

"Fuck!" he mumbled.

He was ready to fight it out, or die trying, when Kreasha stepped in between, signaling him not to do it. When he paused, one of the men spoke up.

"Justice, we come in peace. A mutual friend sent us here to help."

"Who the fuck is this mutual friend?" he shot back.

"We can sit here and chit-chat until the cops run up in this bitch, or we can all get the fuck out of here," the man replied, slightly agitated.

Kreasha and Leneek both nodded their heads to

Justice, telling him to stand down. He sighed and looked at the men standing there fully armed, then gave them the signal.

"Let's move, we have less than five," the man that seemed like the leader shouted.

The other three men that were standing there reacted accordingly, moving in sync as if they had done this plenty of times before. They gently placed Supreme on a stretcher, then connected his cords to a portable monitor.

"Ready for transport," one of them said.

"Follow us, and stay close."

Without saying a word, two of the men cocked their assault mini-machine guns and stepped out of the room ready to lay anything in their way. The other two pushed the stretcher with Supreme on it, while Justice, Kreasha, and Leneek followed closely behind. Any officer they saw was immediately eliminated.

Just as they made out the back entrance, an ambulance was waiting. They loaded Supreme inside; Kreasha never left his side. Justice and Leneek rode in the black SUV that followed behind them. A roadblock was set up by the police on Spruce Street, blocking them from making it to the expressway. The lead car took care of it with a rocket launcher.

"Holy shit, did you see that?" Leneek asked.

"I don't know who the fuck they are, but I'm definitely loving this shit. These motherfuckers are about their business," Justice said.

Once they were on I-76, it was smooth sailing. By the time they made it to I-95, they had eluded all the state troopers. They made it to Delaware in about an hour. Once there, they took Supreme to a secluded location so he could rest. Justice still didn't know who had just helped them, but he was surely grateful. The carnage they left behind would be talked about for years to come.

~ ~ ~

"Is y'all straight?" Justice asked Leneek and Kreasha. They both said yeah. "Leneek, good looking on that situation. You proved your loyalty for real today."

"Did you ever doubt it?"

"No! It's just that, we've done made so many enemies, you never know who you can trust. It's really true what they say, huh: "More money, more problems."

"You don't have to worry about that with me. We in this shit together," Leneek said sincerely.

There was no secret that she had a crush on Justice. If given the chance, she probably would fuck him or Supreme. Maybe both at the same damn time. At the age of twenty-one, Leneek was drop-dead gorgeous. She was five foot five and 125 pounds, with a caramel complexion and 36C chest. What she lacked in the ass department, she made up everywhere else. All and all, if you had to rate her from 1 to 10, she would easily be an 8.5.

"I'm going to call Gabby and Chris to make sure they're straight. They need to be on point about what's going on."

Justice was about to make his call, when a Puerto Rican girl walked into the room. She was dressed in a maid's uniform, but she made it look sexy as hell. It was cut off at the knee and fitted snuggly around the waist. Justice's dick literally stood at attention at the sight of her curvaceous body.

"Mr. Salazar would like to speak with you now," she said with a smile.

"You want me to roll with you?" Leneek asked.

"No! I got this, but thanks."

Justice followed the maid, constantly staring at her ass bouncing back and forth. She led him into a large oval room that was decked out with what seemed to be hundreds of encyclopedias and other lavish items. Justice was amazed at the crystal chandelier hanging from the ceiling, and the expensive pictures hanging on the walls. The room looked like something straight out of a mob movie. After pouring him a drink, the lady stepped out to let the men talk.

"I'm glad to see that you're in one piece, my friend," Ray stated, standing up and shaking Justice's hand. "When your brother Chris saved my sister, I felt that it was only right that I reciprocate the gesture. You and your family are well protected here. I can assure you of that."

"Ray, thank you so much for the hospitality and looking out for us, but I still need to make sure Chris and my girl are safe," Justice said before taking a sip of his drink.

"They are very safe, my friend. As a matter of fact, they should be arriving here shortly," Ray replied, checking his watch.

"Ray, you are something else," Justice stated, smiling from ear to ear. Getting back to the matter at hand, he looked Ray dead in the eyes. "Who's responsible for this?"

Ray leaned back in his chair, then pressed a button on his intercom. He said something to the person on the other end in Spanish, then released the button.

"Have you ever heard of a group called 'the Organization'?"

"No, but are they responsible for my twin brother laying in a coma?"

"They are," he stated, not trying to sugarcoat anything. Just then, a female walked in with a folder in her hand. She passed the folder to Ray then exited the room as quickly as she entered. "Take a look at this. You're not dealing with just any ordinary group of people. These are some very vindictive motherfuckers."

Justice took the folder and looked through it. When he looked at the pictures and names that went along with it, he became angry.

"This is all the information on them?"

"That is everything you would need to retaliate against them. Addresses of all their relatives in the immediate area, what kind of car they drive, where their children go to school, it's all there. Keep in mind that they are law enforcement, politicians, and other high-ranking officials. They have the law on their side, but we have street law on ours."

"I'm going to murder every last one of them," Justice said, closing the folder and placing it on the table.

"You're gonna need some help, my friend. That's why I made a call, and you will have all the soldiers you will need to assist you in your mission. They will be arriving here in two days. Until then, Justice, all I want you to do is get your mind right and keep your brother company. You and your family are welcome to stay here as long as you like."

"Once again, thank you for your hospitality, but I'm gonna pass on staying here. However, I would like you to keep Preme here until all of this is over."

"Anything for you. You will have access to come and go as you please. I will have my sister show you around so you can get familiar with everything. Any weaponry you'll need is in my armory. My only request is, whatever you use out there, don't bring back here."

"Say no more," Justice replied. The two men stood up and shook hands. Justice was already formulating a plan in his head on how he would pay each one of those shystie motherfuckers back, and it wasn't going to be pretty.

SIX

K nock! Knock!

"Yeah," Justice said. When he answered the door, Leneek was standing there.

"Surprise," Neek said, staring at him wearing a towel and nothing else.

"What are you doing here? You supposed to be at Ray's crib until tomorrow. Where are Gabby and them?"

"They're all still there. Seeing that look in your eyes before you left made me come here to make sure you were straight. If you're going after those motherfuckers that did this to Preme, then I'm going with you. There's nothing you can say to make me change my mind."

Justice didn't have anything to say, so he stepped to the side and let her in. He walked past her, heading toward the bathroom.

"Make yourself comfortable while I take a bath. Let me know if you need anything," he said.

"Justice, wait a second," she said, walking toward him. When he turned around, she was standing right in front of him. "I need you to make me feel good, if only for tonight. Tomorrow is war time."

Justice stared at her momentarily. Looking at her body made him realize he hadn't had any pussy in a week. His lil man reassured him of his lack of affection and tried breaking out of the towel. She noticed it and kissed him.

"I see you trying to get it popping," Justice said when she released him.

"We both need this. We're both grown and can hold water, so Gabby won't find out."

"Come chill in the tub with me for a while."

She walked in front of him, and Justice grabbed

her from behind, kissing and nibbling on her neck. He reached around and began to unbutton her blouse. The silky material slid down her arms, and chills filled her body as she felt the warmth of his breath tantalize her skin.

"Ummm," she moaned.

"Shhhhh! I'm only picking with you right now," he whispered into the crook of her neck and shoulder. He dropped his towel and stepped into the hot steamy water.

Leneek unbuttoned her pants and let them hit the floor. Justice unsnapped her bra then reached around and caressed her breasts. His rock-hard dick pressed between her cheeks, causing an instant moistening between her thighs. She stepped out of her panties then turned around and slipped her tongue down his throat. They stood naked and on fire as their hands and mouths explored all the sweet familiarities. Justice lifted her into the tub with him.

"Come on in, the water is fine," he told her.

Justice took his time caressing and rubbing the cloth all over her body. He slowly washed every inch of her, massaging her muscles along the way. This was something he always did for Gabby, and the thought almost made him feel guilty until his thug mentality kicked in. Leneek put her head back and enjoyed the soothing feeling as he made her whole body feel worthy of every touch.

When she was totally relaxed, Justice pulled her into his arms and rested her head against his chest. He slid his hand between her thighs, biting into her neck and circling her clit with his finger, setting her pussy ablaze.

"Mmmmmm," she moaned as she felt his fingers push inside her.

"Cum for me, baby," he whispered in her ear as her head rested on his shoulder.

"Damn, nigga," she cried out as he brought her to

the edge of ecstasy.

"Give it to me." He pressed on her clit and circled faster.

"You want it, take it, motherfucker," she replied, trying to be hard.

Not able to hold it any longer, she gripped the edge of the tub and released her liquids. They came down in a heavy constant flow that made her dizzy. Leneek laid her head to the side and tried to recover as he rubbed slowly up and down her pulsating lips. Justice reached over and gripped her breasts in his hand and squeezed her nipples with the tip of his fingers.

"Yes, be gentle," Leneek whispered, finally letting down her guard. All that hard shit she was talking before went out the door.

"Oh, now you trying to make me be gentle, huh?" His voice was thick with passion. "Lift up before I hold you down and make you do what I want you to do." He stepped out of the tub.

"You trying to put me out of commission," she said with a sexy grin.

Justice lifted her up then pulled Leneek to her feet. He grabbed a towel off the rack and dried her off, touching and caressing her body along the way. Leneek could tell that he was treating her like she was Gabby, and went with the flow, enjoying herself. After tucking the towel around her chest, he grabbed another one and dried himself. He lifted her up and carried her light ass into the guess bedroom, not wanting to disrespect his girl by fucking in their bed. That was one of his rules when bringing a chick to his crib.

He placed several kisses on her stomach, then cupped his arms under her legs and pulled her sweetness to his lips. Leneek pressed her head deep into the pillow as his tongue began to glide over her clit with the lightness of a feather. Placing her hands on his head, she prepared herself for the passionate kiss of his mouth on her twat.

"Just," she whispered.

He dared not answer and lose contact with her sweet pearl, so he just lightly hummed and sucked as her legs began to tremble. Leneek twitched as Justice ran his tongue between her lips, then buried it inside of her.

"Oh my God," she cried out as she tried to wiggle away from his grasp. Justice came up, placing himself over her, and positioning his dick at her opening. "I want to taste me on your lips."

She pulled him up to her and hungrily kissed him as he slid inside her slowly, each inch of his dick filling her to the core. Leneek got lost in the passion as she anticipated each stroke. Every time he pulled back, she craved to have him back inside of her. She closed her eyes and enjoyed him going hard and deep. Justice ran the tip of his tongue over her erect nipples as he answered her cries for more heat.

"Damn, your pussy feels so fucking good," Justice mumbled as she moved just right beneath him.

"I know," she cooed.

"If you know, then throw this pussy at me, baby," he moaned as he began to release deep inside her. "I'm cuummmmin, ohhhh shiitttt."

Leneek spread her legs wider and moved in harmony with him. Justice kissed and sucked her lips as she held him tight. Between her embrace he jerked with excitement. Leneek felt like she was in heaven.

"That was probably the best dick I had in a minute. We definitely have to do this again. Maybe when this shit is all over with," Leneek said, rubbing his chest.

He stuck a finger inside her pussy, then placed it in her mouth, letting her taste both of their orgasms mixed together. She began jerking his dick until it came to life, then stuck it in her mouth, devouring it like a lollipop. Once he was back to full erection, Leneek climbed on top and rode him like a wild stallion. Ten minutes later they were both erupting simultaneously again. They ended up falling asleep in each other's arms.

SEVEN

D etective Robert Pino was sitting in the kitchen drinking a cup of coffee while reading the morning paper. He was waiting for the kids to get ready so he could drop them off at school before he headed to work. He was about to get up and pour himself another glass of coffee, when someone emerged from the corner of the kitchen, brandishing a chrome .44 Bulldog.

"What the fuck is this?" Robert asked.

"Shut the fuck up, nigga," the masked man said, smacking him in the face with the butt of the gun. Robert immediately grabbed his face.

A couple seconds later, three other people came storming in the room with four hostages. They made them kneel on the ground in front of Robert. He watched in horror as his wife, brother, and two kids were held at gunpoint.

"First let me show you that we mean business," the man with the .44 stated. He aimed the gun at the man's head. "Say goodbye!" Without hesitation he pulled the trigger.

"Nooooo!" Robert screamed.

"Now, I hear you're part of the infamous group called the Organization? I want to know, who shot my brother?"

"I didn't have anything to do with that, I swear to God, please don't do this."

"Don't fucking lie to me," the raspy voice boomed as blood red eyes peered down at him.

"I didn't have anything to do with it. How many times do I have to say it?" he yelled from the other end of the Bulldog. "I don't even know who you are."

The man with the gun pulled off his mask revealing his true identity. Robert felt like he was about to puke on himself when he saw Justice standing there. The other three people removed their mask also.

"Do you think we in the habit of putting a gun in the wrong person's face?" Justice smacked Robert across the mouth with his gun, then put it in between his eyes. "Your memory feeling jogged yet, motherfucker?"

"Maybe we need to give him a real reason to mourn," Chris stated.

Chris cocked one in the chamber, then pointed at his wife's head. That gesture got Robert's attention.

"Wait," he yelled out from his kneeled position.

He looked down at his little brother's dead body beside him. Blood ran out of the hole behind his ear, and onto the floor, turning the thick white carpet a crimson red. They had killed him with no purpose other than to show their viciousness. On the other side of Robert, his wife and kids were faced down with a pump shotgun aimed at the back of their heads. Robert knew none of them would be shown any mercy, so he refused to cooperate with any of their demands. If he told these goons anything about the Organization, they would kill him.

"Get it how y'all live," he said, staring death in the face and refusing to tuck his tail.

Leneek was usually the one who stayed in the background and watched over everyone's shoulder, but not this time. She stepped forward and blew the front of Robert's head to the back. When his body twisted and fell to the side, Chris looked up with disgust. They had not gotten any of the information they needed, plus they had stayed a few minutes too long.

Justice grabbed Robert's daughter by her ponytail and pulled her head back so she was staring into those blood-red eyes. She was so paranoid that she peed on herself.

"Bitch, I don't have a problem killing a woman, especially when it comes to my brother," he warned. "I'm gonna ask you one time because I know you know who shot my brother. If you don't give me a name, I'ma let this trigger scream, and you can say goodbye to your daughter, then your son. As you watch their lifeless bodies move on to the afterlife, I'm gonna blow your brains out also." He shoved the gun up under the terrified girl's nose. "Start bumping your gums, bitch."

"They don't tell me nothing. All I do is count the money that he brings home every day," she stuttered.

"Where's the money at?" Justice asked.

"It's in the basement."

Justice pulled her up to her feet by her hair and led her toward the basement stairs. Leneek followed with her pump cocked and ready to cause more carnage. Chris ran Robert's pockets in search of his cellphone. It didn't matter to them who shot Supreme, because all of them involved was gonna die. They just wanted the trigger man so they could torture him and make him suffer more than ever. Once Chris had the phone, he put an insurance shot straight through the man's heart. He stepped over his body and did Robert's brother just as dirty as he had done him. He then proceeded downstairs to assist his friends.

When Chris stepped in the basement, Leneek was tying the kids and their mother up, and Justice was filling the duffle bags sitting on the floor, with the money from the safe. Chris's eyes widened at all the stacks of money that sat in the safe. They hadn't come there for money, but it definitely was a bonus. Leneek stayed there watching the hostages as Chris and Justice carried the duffle bags up the steps.

"Kill that bitch and let's go," Justice yelled over his shoulder.

"What about the kids?" Leneek asked.

Justice looked at her like she was crazy. Even though they were too young to remember anything, his model was "no witnesses, no conviction." After staring at her, Leneek got the picture and nodded her head. Justice continued out of the basement, leaving her to finish the job.

SUPREME & JUSTICE 3

As they threw the bags in the trunk, he heard three shots go off. Less than a minute later, Leneek came storming out of the house.

"Let's go. There's still plenty more to go," Justice said as they all jumped inside the car.

~ ~ ~

Justice parked a few houses down from his destination. The street appeared to be quiet and still, which served him perfectly. He screwed the silencer on the end of his burner, slipped it into his jacket pocket, and headed toward the door.

Justice didn't see the car of the person he was looking for in the driveway, but that didn't deter him one bit. He walked up on the porch and knocked lightly on the door. As he waited for someone to answer, he turned sideways to watch the street and the door at the same time. If that motherfucker happened to pull up, he was going to leave his cabbage well cooked.

"Who is it?" a female called out from behind the

door.

"FedEx! I have a package for Ms. Lindsey Giddish," Justice replied, stepping in front of the peephole so she could see him. He was wearing a FedEx uniform to disguise himself.

He heard her disengage the lock; then she opened the door. Justice stared in her emerald eyes for a second, then at the rest of her body, thinking what a waste of some potentially good pussy.

"How are you? My sister isn't here right now, but I'll sign for it," she said. "Can you bring it in and sit it on the table for me please?"

"Um, I don't know if I want to come in," he said, looking down at the gun in her hand.

"Why not? I don't bite," she replied flirtatiously. Then her eyes followed his, and she realized what he was staring at. "Oops, I don't need this for you, but I gotta be careful being in this big-ass house by myself."

She sat the gun on the picture stand by the door

and smiled at the FedEx employee. He stepped inside and followed her to the den. As they neared the room, he could hear music playing in the living room. He sat the box down and eased his hand in his pocket and quietly slipped his burner out.

As they entered the den, he raised his arm and shot Lindsey's sister in the back of the head. It was so quick that she never saw it coming.

PWWWT!

The silencer muffled the sound but did nothing to limit the damage. Her pretty blond streaked tresses puffed out around her head like a halo. Blood and skull matter sprayed out of her forehead, and she crashed to the floor on her face.

"Stupid bitch!" he said.

Justice pumped two more slugs into her then stepped over her body, took a seat on the couch, and fired up a blunt that he found on the end table. As the smoke filled his lungs, he waited for his next victim to come home and walk into his death trap. All of a sudden, a sinister look came over his face. He walked over to where Lindsey's sister's body lay lifeless on the floor, and removed her shorts and panties. He stood over the top of her licking his lips, with lust in his eyes. Justice walked away, and when he came back, he kneeled down behind her body.

"Might as well have some fun while I'm waiting," he said out loud to no one in particular. With that said he shoved the broom handle up her ass, pushing it as far as it could go. If she was still breathing, she would be in so much pain. He plunged and plunged until his arm got tired, then stood up, leaving the broom dangling from her hole.

~ ~ ~

Lindsey came into the house with a bag full of money slung over her shoulder. She had just collected it from one of their many establishments owned by the Organization. Lindsey had to admit that her lifestyle had become so much easier since joining them. She was getting paid from both sides and making off like a bandit. They were the ones funding everything that dealt with taking the top dealers off the streets. If you weren't working for or with them, then you were their enemy. They were extorting everybody from Philadelphia to Washington DC.

Their political gang stretched over five different states, and counting. The reason no one ever knew about them was because up until now, they were very discrete about who they included in their operation. No one knew who the bigwigs were, or so they thought.

"Kathy," Lindsey called out as she followed the sound of the music that was coming from the living room. "Come help me divide this money before I go back to work."

When she stepped into the room, she saw her sister stretched out on the floor in an unnatural twist, with a broom handle sticking out of her asshole. She froze in her spot and pulled out her police-issued

Glock, then bent over to see if her sister was dead.

"Bet you didn't think that today would be your last day on this planet, did you?" the voice said from behind.

Lindsey turned and looked up. She never even had a chance to react, because the last thing she saw before being sent to join her sister was the person she thought was on his dying bed.

PWWT! PWWT! PWWT!

Justice stepped back admiring his handiwork. The corners of his mouth formed into an evil smirk. Two down and a lot more to go. It was only a matter of time before they were going to start striking back. It was time to gather up the men that Ray had at his disposal, and hit them where it hurts. He tucked his gun, grabbed the money that she had come in with, and eased out of the house without anyone seeing him.

As he headed back to Ray's estate to check on his brother, he thought about how each person he killed had bags of cash in their cribs. This was bigger than he thought, and they were very well connected.

~ ~ ~

After talking to Justice on the phone, Chris needed a change of clothes, so he went home to grab some things. He wanted to hurry back before Justice came because they were about to turn all the way up. He hit the remote and pulled into the garage. He waited for the garage door to come down before exiting his vehicle. When he stepped inside the house, he snatched the cigarillo that was filled with loud, and sparked it up.

He sat down on the couch to relax for a while, when his cellphone rang. He checked the screen and saw that it was this jump-off he been fucking for a while.

"Yizzo," he replied, answering the call.

"My kitty is purring right now for some affection, babe."

"I have some business to take care of right now,

but when I'm done I'll swing over there," Chris told the lil freak.

"I need you over here now to take the place of my finger. It's not working, and I'm so wet right now. I really need some dick right now, Chris," she demanded.

"Listen, business before pleasure, and right now I'm wasting too much time talking to you. If you can't wait, find another dick to satisfy you."

"I just might do that," the chick said, ending the call in his ear. Chris just laughed knowing that she was telling the truth because she was the neighborhood slut.

He leaned back on the couch and finished smoking the loud. The feeling had him calm and ready to murder anything or anyone that got in his way. He had to hurry up and change, so he got up and headed for the stairs. As he made his way toward the bedroom, someone was waiting in the hallway closet. The intruder crept up behind him and put the gun to the back of his head. Chris was stunned and caught off guard at the same time.

"What's going on? What is this about?" he asked, with his hands in the air.

"Y'all should've left well enough alone." That was the last words he heard.

BOC! BOC!

EIGHT

*I*t had been over an hour since Chris was supposed to meet them back at Ray's estate. Justice and Kreasha were sitting by Supreme's bed, watching the private nurse checking his vital signs and the IV he was attached to. She was making sure his body was receiving the proper amount of nutrition. Justice hit Chris's number back to back, and each time he was sent straight to voicemail. When he tried to reach Leneek, her phone sent him to voicemail too.

"What the fuck is going on?" he wondered out loud.

"Is everything okay?" Kreasha asked, watching Justice's facial expression.

"Yeah," he replied back, but wasn't so sure.

He tried reaching out to them again, and still there was no answer. Now he was really becoming concerned. He immediately called Whoopie, and after four rings, he finally got an answer.

"What's up, boss?" Whoopie slurred.

"Where you at?"

"At the crib. What's going on? You straight?" Whoopie suddenly came to attention hearing the urgency in Justice's voice.

"Is your girl with you?"

"Yeah, she's sitting next to me. Why? What's up?" Whoopie got off the sofa and walked into the other room, closing the door behind him. Leneek sat up, then got off the sofa and walked close to the door to try and catch what was going on.

"You seen or heard from Chris?" Justice asked as he stepped out of the room and headed down the hall to the guest room where he made Kreasha stay.

"Not since earlier, when he said he was going to stop by the crib to change clothes. Why? What's up, bro? Talk to me."

"I don't know yet, but be ready so you don't have

to get ready, and be on standby. Put the crew on point. We might have to turn this city upside down."

"Done!" Whoopie hung up and called every last one of their team leaders and informed them to have everyone on standby. When he called Devon, he could hear him getting some head.

"Yo, get on point, homie," Whoopie stated, causing Devon to end his oral pleasure with the lil bitch that not too long ago was trying to link up with Chris. "I'll be there to snatch you up in a few minutes."

Leneek heard the doorknob turn and ran back and hopped on the couch. Whoopie didn't even look in her direction as he moved to the closet and pulled out the black duffle bag containing his armory.

"Babe, what's the matter?" she asked, looking worried.

"Nothing," Whoopie said, grabbing his vest and throwing it on before throwing his hoodie on overtop.

"Whoopie, don't lie to me. I know the code. What happened? I rock out for my nigga Just, and he knows I put in work."

"We need you to stay put while we handle this shit real quick. Don't open the door for anybody, not even me." He looked at her with a firm eye.

"Whoopie, what the fuck?"

"Chill, ain't shit going on yet that I know of, but we are at war. These motherfuckers don't care about shit, okay! Just be on alert and stop asking me the same question when I don't answer. It's for a reason." He strapped up then reached under the sofa and detached his baby snug from the bottom. He leaned in and kissed Leneek on the lips, then rolled out.

Leneek grabbed her cellphone and called Justice. She was sent straight to voicemail. She tried again with the same result.

"What the fuck is going on?" she said aloud, then hopped up and threw on some clothes. Just as she was stepping into her boots, her phone rang beside her.

~ ~ ~

Justice moved around the room hitting Chris's phone every few minutes. His mind began producing flashes of all the torture he had been putting on the streets and the danger that was yet to come. The enemy had the upper hand because they wore the badges, but he refused to go out without putting up a fight. That was out of the question. If dying was his destiny, so be it!

"I'll be right back," he said, rushing toward the door.

"Where you going? I just ordered your food," Kreasha said, walking toward him. Kreasha was no fool. She could see the seriousness in Justice's demeanor, and a sinking feeling moved in her chest. "Babe, you okay?"

"Yeah, I'm good. Just chill until I get back. I just have to check on something."

"You promise?" she asked, looking in his eyes, hoping that he didn't get hurt out there. She knew what was going on, but she was a female, so she was going to always worry about her man's wellbeing.

"Yeah, ma, I promise that I will always come back to you," Justice reached out and took her in his arms. "Don't eat all my food," he joked.

"Shut up. You better hurry up back," she replied, squeezing him tightly.

When Justice heard a small whimper and felt her hand settle on his lower back, he kissed the top of her head. He tried to inform her that her nigga was built for whatever, and that she didn't have to worry about him.

"You good, ma, just let me handle this. I'll be back. You're safe in this fortress, and look at the squad of goons I have with me. They're not letting anyone get close to me."

When he hopped in the car, the first thing he did was call Gabby, because she hadn't come back yet.

She was supposed to pick up her stuff and come back. Even though she had four soldiers with her, he still wanted to check on her.

"Hey, baby," Gabby said.

"I was just making sure that you were straight."

"Yes, I just got out the shower, and I was going to take a nap until you come get me."

"You know where the heat is, right?"

"Yes."

"Bring it downstairs, and don't hesitate to use it," he said. "If you feel threatened in any way and the guards don't get there in time, shoot first and ask questions last."

Gabby understood exactly what he meant. When he was off the phone, she put the chain on the door, then sat on the loveseat and fell asleep.

~ ~ ~

Whoopie arrived at Devon's house in full kill mode. He stepped out of his truck and walked up to the porch. When he knocked on the door, Isaiah opened it. He was dressed in all black, and a hoodie was pulled over his head. Whoopie's breathing was quick and intense, causing Isaiah to look at him strangely.

"No word from Just yet?" Isaiah asked, moving to the side.

"Nah, I want you to head over to Preme's house and pick the work up that's in the basement. We have to get that stuff up out of there because it's only a matter of time before the feds gonna come knocking at the door."

"A'ight. What about Leneek?"

"She straight," Whoopie said confidently.

Isaiah grabbed his burner and headed out the door. Devon was seated on the couch taking a few shots of Cîroc to the head and loading his whistle. Whoopie took a seat adjacent to his and took his cellphone out and placed it on the table. He stared at it for a minute then sat back and waited for the next move. He was hoping for the best, but preparing for the worst.

~ ~ ~

Gabby jumped when she heard the doorbell. Her first instinct was to go upstairs and get one of the guns. Then she remembered that the four soldiers were outside. When she looked through the peephole, one of the men was standing there. She thought maybe he had to use the bathroom. She unlocked the door and opened it up.

BOOM!

The loud bang of the gunshot rang her ears, and the man's brains splashed all over her face. His body lurched forward before crumbling down across her feet. Gabby screamed.

"Shut the fuck up, bitch!" barked the hooded figure, raising the gun up to her face.

Gabby's eyes grew wide with fear as she stared at the weapon. She slowly stepped back, but the intruder stepped with her. The cool air whipped in the door causing her gown to blow. The eyes at the other end of the gun were unaffected though.

"What do you want?" she asked in a frightened tone. "Please, you can have whatever you want. I didn't see anything." She continued to slowly back into the house.

"Bitch, I don't want shit you got except your life."

Gabby looked at the eyes of her assassin, and the heat drained from her body. She felt wetness trickle down her inner thigh, settling in a puddle under her feet. A haunting laugh came in her direction; then she heard bullets being bumped into the chamber. That really made her get nervous as the attacker lowered the gun toward her stomach.

"Please, I'm pregnant," she cried, covering her belly with both hands.

Gabby was supposed to surprise Justice with the news that she was pregnant, but never had the chance to.

"Yes, I know!"

BOOM! BOOM!

"Noooooo!" she screamed as the first bullet tore through her left hand, cracking her ring and entering high in her abdomen. The second bullet shattered her hip bone.

Gabby fell back into the end table, knocking the lamp over as her body crashed to the floor. Her heart beat fast as she tried to crawl away from the deliverer of death. She placed her hand on her stomach and began to shake when she saw all the blood that coated her palm.

"My baby," she cried.

"Take that little bastard with you to the afterlife," the coldhearted assassiness sneered. Then the intruder stood over her and shot her in her beautiful face. "Die, bitch," she spat and shot Gabby again before turning and fleeing out the door.

Gabby lay whimpering on the floor. She tried to move, but her legs no longer worked. When she tried to lift her head, blood filled her eyes and stole her vision. She wanted to cry out, but thick warm blood filled her mouth and choked off her cries. As darkness began to envelope her, Gabby gave up the fight. She was ready to give in to the eerie silence of death.

"Help me," she moaned.

And with her final breath, her thoughts left her and the baby, and instead she prayed that Supreme and Justice would have the strength to send all their enemies' souls to hell.

NINE

*M*ayor Street sat at the head of the conference table in the office of one of the Organization's nightclubs. He had his hands folded atop the table. He looked around the room at the other men present. Agent Pryor and her partner Agent Roman sat to the right of him. Deputy Mayor Catrena Alston and her top lieutenant, Tony Denoza were on the left. The mayor's newly elected street general Dean was posted by the door, looking like a model with his low-cut, wavy hair. Many had mistaken his pretty-boy, business-minded demeanor for softness. As a result of underestimating his gangsta, they ended up getting fitted for a casket.

Not only was Dean the head of security at the club, but he was also a stone-cold murderer. He had added a half dozen bodies to his street resume since hooking up with the mayor two years ago. When the mayor hired him to take out their biggest competition, Dean was more than willing to oblige. This was his chance to prove that he was more than just some security guard, and he hoped that the mayor would give him an even bigger and better position.

As Dean looked around the room at the other men and women, he decided that anyone that bucked the agenda was getting carried out of there wrapped up in a sheet. He made eye contact with the mayor and received the silent okay.

Sitting beside Mayor Street, Agent Pryor wore an expression of deep agitation. She unconsciously fiddled with her signature small diamond earrings that hung from her earlobes, and released a heavy sigh. Two of her friends had gotten killed the other night, and others were lying in hospitals fighting losing battles for their lives.

In addition to those problems, she had a huge

shipment due to arrive today, and a feeling of angst had her by the throat. Normally she wouldn't be caught dead in the same room with Dean, but Mayor Street had convinced her that he would be a valuable asset to them all.

Her real threat was somewhere mourning the death his of stepbrother and wife right now, so she really wasn't worried about Dean right now. Agent Pryor could barely hold his tongue as she sat waiting to see what the mayor could tell her to calm her anxiety. Another person in the room, named Ab, was seething too. In the last couple of days, his nephew and one of his workers had gotten gunned down outside of a store on 52nd and Spruce. Then this morning one of his main runners stepped out of the house and caught a chest full of lead. Bodies were dropping all around the city, and Justice was behind the killings. He had a team from out of town that killed for fun, and they were very well trained like they were in the military. He needed to be dealt with before he became an even powerful force.

Before today, Ab would've never considered joining forces with some damn cops. Right now though, they made him a deal he couldn't turn down. He was able to move dope all over the city as long as he helped them kill Justice and his team. He informed them that Justice had a twin brother. That was something nobody knew, not even the feds. It all started to make sense to them now. This other twin was out for justice, and they were the targets.

Sometimes Catrena wished she never had joined the Organization and that they would have handled this the right way instead of like vigilantes. It was too late now, there was no turning back from this. Being with them had its perks because everyone associated with the Organization was rich and untouchable. That was until they fucked with the wrong person.

Ab stared at the bottles of liquor and the spread of cold cuts that sat untouched in the center of the table as he tried to comprehend why a motherfucker he never had beef with had declared war on him. He didn't care because he was going to send some heat right back at that ass. If this meeting was about anything other than killing Justice, he was out.

Deputy Mayor Alston took a drink, then stood up. She cleared her throat, and all heads turned in her direction, ready to get this meeting underway.

"Ladies and gentlemen, we have a problem," she began, walking around the table.

"You're goddamn right we do," Tony exploded as he shot to his feet, slamming his palms down on the table so hard that the liquor bottles rattled together.

Ab stood up next to his boss and slid his hand inside his jacket where his tool was tucked in a shoulder holster.

"Nigga, sit your ass down before I shatter your motherfucking spine!" The voice on the back of Tony's neck belonged to the quiet assassin Dean.

Ab let his hand fall to his side but remained

standing in defiance. The only smell of pussy on him was on the tip of his dick. He had been through so many battles, and had the scars all over his body and soul to prove it. A few years ago a fierce rival had doused him with gasoline and set him on fire. Ab had lived through that to come back and torture the nigga in the same hideous fashion, so a ratchet in the center of his back was nothing to him.

Dean knew of Ab's reputation, but he was not impressed. Yeah, he had recovered and burned that nigga to death, but if it would've been him, Dean would've eradicated that motherfucker's entire bloodline behind that shit. Every time he looked in the mirror and saw those scars, he would've gone out and killed another member of that nigga's family, he told himself as he waited for Ab to give him a reason to send his back flying out of his chest.

Mayor Street shook his head, letting Dean know to turn shit down, this wasn't the time for that type of beef. Dean nodded and backed away, but he kept his stare trained on Ab's back.

"Gentlemen, please be seated. This is exactly what this kid Justice wants to happen," Catrena said in a calm voice.

She reluctantly sat back down, and after a pause, Ab did the same. She knew Dean was gonna end up killing him.

Agent Roman sat quietly taking in everything around him. He was a thinker, and only took sides with the stronger team. He hadn't made it this far doing what he did without being able to read his friends as well as his foes.

Catrena poured herself another glass of vodka, then lifted the glass to her lips and tossed it back all in one gulp.

"Ahhh," she let out as it burned the back of her throat. She sat the glass down and rubbed her hands together. When she was sure she held their attention, she spoke with no preamble. "As we all can see, we have one enemy in common, and we need to get rid of them before they get the rest of us. I would think that it's in all of our best interest to come together and take them out. No more of this beefing with each other. Are we clear on this?"

"That's what a lot of other people were supposed to do, and look how that turned out," Agent Pryor mumbled loud enough for everyone to still hear her.

"Not good," Tony interjected with a shrug of his shoulders; that didn't sit well with Dean. He had lost over twenty soldiers to Justice and his crew.

"Why don't you just let us send a bunch of agents in there and put them behind bars?"

"That's not gonna work because all that will happen is one of them high-priced lawyers will get them off once again," the mayor responded, tired of hearing the nonsense. "It's like those assholes are untouchable or something."

"I told you if we missed they would come back at us with everything they got," Catrena chimed in. "How the hell do they know who did it?"

"There's no way Justice could have known that you were in on that because only the Organization knew about it."

"It's obvious that we have a leak within the Organization, and we need to bring them to the forefront ASAP," Mayor Street replied.

"You think our asset is involved with this? Maybe even playing both sides?"

"If so, then you know what to do."

"It sounds to me like you all are shook."

Tony was offended but hid it nicely. When this was over he was going to kill Agent Roman. He suspected him of having one of his shipments knocked off.

"I'm not afraid of no man. Let's send somebody after him that won't miss. I don't have time for this shit," he remarked, glancing down at his watch. "In two hours he's supposed to meet his connect to receive the shipment. That is the time to catch him because he don't travel that deep when he goes there."

"This is different, they will be strapped up crazy because of his men and that chick of Supreme's getting touched. He won't be traveling alone this time, that's for sure."

"Let our asset know that the price is now triple for both of the twins' heads," the mayor said.

Ab stared at Dean, sending the message to their asset. He never took his eyes off of him the whole time he was texting. When he was done and noticed him staring, he had to say something.

"You got something you wanna say?"

"I just want to know who these niggas are, and how they just popped up out of nowhere causing so much havoc? It's like one day these niggas names started ringing in the streets, and next thing I know he's killing motherfuckers."

"He didn't come out of nowhere, I found out that he was running with the nigga Walid until he got smoked. Now he's running with some fucking cartel that don't take no shit from anyone."

"You can bet they took him under their wing, 'cause he don't move like the average dope dealer."

As the agent talked, they could hear the contempt in his voice as he talked about the cartel Justice and his team had joined. They were so dangerous that the FBI was even hesitant when it came to going up against them.

For some strange reason Dean could sense that he was holding back on some information that could maybe shed some light on this infamous group.

"Why don't you give us the uncut version of these niggas since we're the ones that will be going at them."

The Organization discussed strategies on getting Justice and his crew. The meeting lasted for another forty-five minutes before everyone left. Mayor Street and Deputy Mayor Alston stayed back holding a conference call with their close friend, the director of the FBI.

"We should continue going after his women; that would hurt him a lot."

"But that won't take care of Justice," the director pointed out. "Fuck snatching up bitches to make some nigga feel pain. You have to bring it to their front door, and don't back down. I have a hundred agents on payroll waiting to put in work. Let me know if you need them."

"Will do. I have some work to take care of, so if you need me, I will be back at the office," Catrena said. As far as she was concerned, there was nothing left to talk about. Tomorrow they were going to bring the drama to them, but tonight she was going to let her team relax. When she walked to the door, Tony and Ab were waiting for her. "Take the rest of the night off and enjoy yourself. Call me in the morning and I'll give you the rundown. I'm going to the office to catch up on some work."

"You don't need us to tag along?"

"That won't be necessary," she said, heading out

the back door.

"Fuck that. We're going to hit that nigga tonight. Let's go over to the strip club that he hangs out at," Tony said.

"I'm down," Ab co-signed. He was thinking the same thing, but his smile masked his duplicitous thoughts. They shook hands in agreement.

"Whoever we see up in that bitch tonight, die right there. We're gonna send our own message tonight, bro. Fuck waiting on them to strike at us."

"Don't miss this time," Ab said as they walked out. "We can't afford to screw up."

When they stepped outside, they saw Dean riding by. He stopped in front of them and rolled the window down.

"Later for you, blood!" he said with a smile.

"Nigga, you better concentrate on Justice and his crew, 'cause this right here ain't what you want."

"Says the man that's scared of a lil-ass kid," Dean snickered. He just wanted to see how far he could go before Ab wanted to take a shot at the title.

Ab put his fingers to his mouth and blew him the kiss of death. But somebody should have warned all of them that Justice would require all of their attention, and he would not be their only worry. One of the cruddiest niggas alive was just waiting to put in some work. This nigga was on some murder, death, kill type time, and he was ready to show them that they were better off fucking with someone else instead of what he had for them.

TEN

ony and Ab headed over to Vanity Grand with the hopes of running into Justice or one of his crew. The club was lit, with so many dancers that Tony couldn't choose which one he wanted to keep him company. As they waited for their drinks, this one chick walked past meeting and greeting the other patrons. Tony grabbed her arm and pulled her toward him.

"I'm trying to see what that be like, sis," he said.

"Put up or shut up!" she fired back. "You know what it is, money talks."

"Then you hearing me loud and clear," Tony replied.

Pulling out a knot of cash, he flashed it at the dancer, then slid it back in his pocket. Tony now had her attention. It was funny how money suddenly changed her perception of him.

"VIP?" she asked.

"Yeah, no doubt!" he replied. "Slow your roll for a minute though. Check it out, it's my man's birthday, and umm, he's trying to do the damn thing."

"What are you trying to do?" the dancer asked.

"We're trying to get some head," he admitted. "You know, like a ménage à trois type of thing, dig me?"

"I hear what you're saying, but do you have ménage à trois money? I hope y'all not like the rest of these broke-ass niggas in here. They talk a good game, and never come up with the bread to make it happen," she countered. "Long as you got the bread, anything is possible."

"Well I just showed you that I have plenty of bread, and you know what they say, everything's negotiable," Tony replied. "Me and my man just

ERNEST MORRIS

trying to get it popping."

To prove he wasn't all talk, and really was trying to get at her, he reached into his other pocket and pulled out a different bankroll of cash. The sight of all that money seemed to stimulate her in ways that sex never could.

"Since you put it that way, let's get it then," she said. "Grab your mans and let's get this party started."

"Say no more!" Tony said with a smirk.

With a wave of the hand, he motioned for his friend to join them. The stripper, who went by the name Sparkle, grabbed the two of them by the hand. She led them through the cramped, dimly lit club, past countless scantily clad strippers, to the VIP lounge. It was there that the beauty planned on relieving the two ballers of some of their easy-come-easy-go cash, and even some hot white lava.

She gave the big husky bouncer posted up outside

the VIP area a wink of the eye, signaling to him that she was going in to handle some business and that she would take care of him when she was done. In exchange, he would turn a blind eye while she performed some lewd sexual acts that were against the club's policy. It seemed like everyone had a hustle in the club, from the strippers to the bartenders. They all had a price. This was how a lot of the bouncers made extra money for themselves, by allowing the girls to perform nothing short of prostitution. One hand washed the other in life, and the same went on in the club.

Once inside the VIP lounge, Sparkle playfully shoved Tony down on the couch, faking aggression. Then she pounced on him. She gave him a view of her ass as she proceeded to grind on him from a reverse cowgirl position. While she sat on Tony's lap, she fondled Ab's nuts. Tony could see that she was the kind of chick that was down for whatever as long as the money was right. Ab rubbed Sparkle's ass cheeks while Tony fondled her breasts. Once she got completely naked, the sight of her body had the two men ready to fuck.

"Yeah, nigga, grip this fat ass. Squeeze that shit. You like it, don't you?" Sparkle said, talking shit to them.

Repositioning herself, she turned to face Tony before sitting back down on his lap. Sparkle began to slowly dry-fuck him, rubbing her pussy back and forth over his erection, working him into a sexual frenzy. Tony was dying of anticipation to get inside her goodies. He needed to see if she could take some dick.

"Okay, before we go any further, let me see that green," she said.

Without a moment's hesitation, Tony quickly reached into his pocket and peeled off a couple of hundreds from his roll.

"Here go mine right here! Ab gone hit you off with his too."

"Come on, baller, I thought you were paying for both being as though it's his birthday," Sparkle said, trying to call his bluff.

Tony almost forgot that he lied and said it was Ab's birthday. He reached into his pocket and pulled out a couple more hundreds and passed the money to her. Sparkle took possession of the money, then removed two condoms from her bag, broke the seal, and popped one into her mouth while holding the other in her hand. In one swift motion, she was on her knees, unfastening both of their pants. She took Tony's dick in her mouth while giving Ab the hand job of a lifetime.

"Ummm," Tony moaned. Sparkle's mouth was hot, wet, and tight, just like a pussy. Even the hand job she was giving Ab had his head spinning. "Damn, you can suck some dick."

"Did you ever doubt me?" she said, removing his manhood briefly from her mouth.

She started sucking on his dick again nonstop, barely getting any air to breathe. Her fellatio expertise was sending chills up Tony's spine. Just as he experienced one wave of pleasure, another one followed. He could have sworn that she had deep-throated his dick, which was quite a feat since he wasn't small in that department.

"Stay just like that," Ab said, positioning himself behind her.

She passed him the condom without even looking back. He slid it on, then slid right into her warm hole. Her pussy was tight as a glove. Each pump had him ready to explode. Suddenly, a jolt of semen raced from his testicles, to the head of his penis, swelling it to twice its normal size. He unloaded his babies safely inside the contraceptive.

"Damn, that pussy was killer!" he proclaimed.

"You can say that again," a voice said from a distance.

Ab turned around and was staring down the barrel of a .40 Cal, equipped with a silencer. Before he could get a word out, two bullets went straight through his forehead. PSSST! PSSST!

"What the fuck is . . ." Sparkle bit down hard on Tony's dick.

"Ahhhhhhh," he screamed out in pain.

"What'd you think, you'd come here and catch me slipping? Nah, nigga, you and your man is the one slipping," Justice said. Everything was starting to spiral out of control for him. Supreme was still in a coma, Chris was missing in action, and he had found out that his girl was murdered in her crib. He asked Ray's connections to find out who was behind it, and they informed him that niggas were about to come for him by any means. Sparkle bit on his genitals again causing him to yelp again like a hog.

"Ughhhhh, tell her to let me go, please," Tony begged.

"Sure, let him go, baby," Justice told her.

As soon as Sparkle let go, Justice kicked Tony in the face. He fell backward onto the couch, holding his head. Justice aimed his gun at his forehead and was ready to pull the trigger, when Tony spoke up.

"Wait, wait, I'll give you all the money, just let me breathe."

"Nah, I'll pass on that, homie. See you in hell, cannon!"

PSSST! The shot entered Tony's forehead and exited out the back, splashing blood all over the back of the couch. He sent two more shots his way, hitting him in the heart area for good measure.

"Call homeboy in here to clean this shit up. You did good, ma," Justice said, squeezing her ass.

"Stop past the crib later tonight and I'll give you my thanks."

"You already know I got this," she replied, caressing his dick. Justice reached into his pocket and pulled out two envelopes. He passed Sparkles the thicker of the two, then headed over to the VIP door. The big burly bouncer stood there, mean mugging everything moving. He gave Justice a head nod as he accepted the envelope from him and tucked it in his back pocket.

"Yizzo, get in here," Sparkle yelled over the loud music.

Once the bouncer walked in and saw the mess, he shook his head. "We have to take care of this ASAP." He paused, listening to his boss over his headset. "The boss said the cleanup crew just arrived, so do me a solid. Wait here and lemme make sure the coast is clear before you go back to the dressing room."

Sparkle had blood on her body, so that wasn't a

problem. She was thinking about what Justice said to her, and was hoping for the chance to finally get in his pants. Carmella had a crush on him ever since they were younger and he was fucking Gabby. They both always flirted with each other, but that was as far as it went. She gave him plenty of dances trying to get him to fuck, but he wouldn't bite. When she heard the niggas plotting on him, she quickly called him and told him what the move was. He told her to stall them out until he got there. That's why she made sure she took them to the special VIP room. The room was soundproof and was made especially for people who came to the club causing trouble or anything like that. The bouncer gave her the signal that she was good. As she was leaving, four men wearing all black passed her carrying two bags. She already knew what they were there to do.

"Later, Bam," she said, tapping his arm.

"Later, sexy, and enjoy your night."

She quickly went back to the dressing room, washed up, and got dressed, then headed home for the night, ten grand richer. When she pulled in front of her door, she parked and hopped out. She went to grab her bag out of the backseat, when someone approached her from behind and slit her throat. Out of reflex, Carmella reached for her throat, trying to stop the bleeding. She tried to turn around to see who cut her, but they were gone. Choking on her own blood, she fell down in the middle of the street. Because it was so late at night, no one was out to save her. A passerby was driving by and noticed her body sprawled out, but it was too late, Carmella was gone.

ELEVEN

*Y*etta was lying in her bed in the hotel, watching a new show on the E channel called *Life of Kylie*. Just as the second one was starting, there was a knock on her door. Yetta opened up the door, thinking it was the person she was waiting for, and was greeted by a pleasant surprise.

Before she could even object, the waiter proceeded to walk in with two bottles of liquor and a large fruit salad. Instantly his eyes became glued to Yetta's tank top and her nipples, which pressed against the thin cotton material of her top. The waiter almost pushed the cart into the wall, he was staring so hard.

"What is this? I didn't order this," she said.

"I did," a male's voice said.

Yetta turned around with a smile on her face.

She thought that he was once again standing her up. He stood there with two glasses in his hand. He had on a baby-blue Armani Exchange button up shirt, a pair of True Religion jeans, and a pair of Vans on his feet.

"That will be all for now," he said, holding up a twenty-dollar bill. The waiter gladly took the money and walked out, wishing that it was him about to share a drink with her.

"I thought you weren't coming," she stated, trying to act like she was calm.

"And miss the chance to spend time with you, never that," he replied. "I had to check on some shit before coming, but now I'm here. Let me pour you a drink."

"Yeah, you do that," Yetta said. "It's the least you could do, being as though you stood me up before."

As he poured two glasses, she studied his

handsome features. Her body began to yearn for him as she thought about what he would do to her. Valiantly, she fought the feeling of jumping on him.

"You wanna make a toast?"

"Don't mind if I do," Yetta said, raising her glass. "Here's to a new alliance."

"And old ones," he added as they clanked their glasses together, then downed the contents.

The two of them laughed, joked, and continued to drink. Without even realizing it, they had downed both bottles of liquor. They both thoroughly enjoyed each other's company. It was a welcome diversion from the tropical storm that was building on the streets.

"Excuse me if I'm out of line, Yetta, but I could just eat you up, girl," he said. "I think I'm letting the liquor talk for me."

Yetta desperately tried not to let that statement go to her head. She knew that he was just trying to spit game, but he didn't need to. She wanted to give him some pussy, but before she did, she had to make sure he was all in on the plan she had put together.

"I think you're right," she joked. "It might be the liquor talking, but I'm intrigued to find out if you can back it up."

"Oh, you best believe I can."

"Before we go any further, let's be clear on something. If what we're doing doesn't work, we are both dead. This is a dangerous game that we're playing, with some very powerful people. I want my brother's empire, and you want to be the new mayor. Together we could be unstoppable and wouldn't have to worry about anyone getting in the way."

"I know what we're risking, so what's the plan?"

"All we have to do is sit back and let them kill each other. Then once the last man is standing, we step in and take them out."

"I couldn't have said it better myself," he replied,

ERNEST MORRIS

walking up on Yetta.

"I love you!"

For a long moment he said nothing. Yetta was trying to get into his head, and hoped that it worked. He just stared back at her momentarily, then smiled.

"Good," he said and kissed her. The kiss was so long and strong that it was hard for either of them to catch their breath.

"Oh damn, baby," Yetta moaned, finally releasing his tongue from hers.

Her body was responding to his slightest touch. He began to kiss, lick, and suck her neck as if his life depended on it. Yetta's body squirmed and moaned from each bite and suck.

"I want you so fucking bad," he growled.

"You can show me better than you can tell me," Yetta boldly stated, slipping out of her wifebeater and wiggling out of her shorts. She lay butt naked, waiting for him to join her. "Hurry up and take

116

what's yours."

"Sssshhh," he replied. "I don't wanna hear nothing but you moaning when I stick this dick up in you."

Suddenly he was on top of her, and they were embracing, kissing, biting, and sucking as if they couldn't get enough of each other. He ran his tongue along the dangerous curves of Yetta's body as his hands roamed freely. He started on her neck, then slowly worked his way down to her shoulders to her erect nipples, down to her belly button where he stopped to thrust his tongue inside.

Yetta moaned and clutched him to her. Pleasure clouded her mind as every part of her being throbbed in anticipation. Watching him lick on her was a turn on itself. Yetta made sex faces as the anticipation and pleasure intensified. Instead of fulfilling Yetta's burning desire to feel his face buried between her thighs, he took an unexpected detour to her manicured toes.

Placing her right foot in his mouth, he sucked her toes like he was possessed. Yetta's back arched as a strong euphoric sensation shot straight through her body. She began to rub her clitoris and was soon overcome by orgasm after orgasm. Never in her twenty-three years on this earth had she experienced something so intense. These were the best orgasms she ever had by this highly experienced man that was ravishing her heated body.

He loved satisfying his partners, getting them off first. It was a turn on for him to see them having an orgasm as a result of something he did. Pushing her legs apart, he had a good view of Yetta's neatly trimmed vagina. She was still recovering from her last orgasm when he once again buried his head between her legs eating her pussy. Yetta's body began to quiver as he nibbled and sucked on her clitoris.

Yetta's moans and screams only excited him. She begged him to stop, but he wouldn't. He knew as well as she did that she really didn't want him to stop. When she tried to pull away from his hungry mouth, he only chased her, locking his arms around her thighs till she couldn't escape. She thrust her hips wildly as she climaxed over and over again. Yetta was unable to take much more of this. Although she was a willing recipient, she was beginning to feel selfish. It was time for her to return the favor.

"Now it's your turn," Yetta said seductively, finally pulling from him. She pushed him onto his back and went straight for his dick.

She took as much of him as she possibly could into her mouth, testing her gag reflexes. Yetta then began going up and down, bobbing her head in a smooth rhythm. Saliva began to ooze from her mouth, saturating him. A few well-timed sighs and moans were her reward for a job well done.

"Oh shit, eat this dick," he moaned. "This shit is bananas."

Yetta sucked his dick so long and hard that her mouth began to dry out. She raised up for a moment and crawled a short distance to the food cart. She removed a bottle of liquor along with a bucket of ice. After popping a few pieces of ice in her mouth, Yetta was right back at it. She commenced to sucking him off with renewed vigor.

The coldness of the ice and the warmth of her mouth drove him crazy. He wanted to tell Yetta to chill, but it was so ridiculously addictive, and somehow the words got lost in his throat. He couldn't talk because he was too busy moaning. Over and over again, she would repeat the process of popping ice in her mouth whenever what she had in her mouth melted. He felt the head of his dick swell up, and was unable to contain himself any longer, nor did he want to.

"Cum in my mouth, baby, please," Yetta whispered, well aware of what was going on. She blew cold air on the tip of his dick, causing him to erupt like a volcano in her mouth.

"Oh my God!" he managed to say.

Yetta wasn't finished yet. Usually he would need a minute to recuperate. However, she wasn't trying to wait. She began to gently suck him until he was fully erect again. Carefully, Yetta spread her legs apart and lowered herself onto his fully erect penis. Her love juices were still flowing, so she was easily able to guide it right in.

She started riding his dick like a true cowgirl, dictating the tempo of the sex. Up and down she went, getting it just how she liked it, hard and fast. They were so far gone that they weren't even thinking about the unprotected sex they were engaged in, that could lead to pregnancy or a disease. The thought would undoubtedly cross their minds later, but for now they were adhering to the pleasure principle.

Sweat dripped off their bodies as Yetta went from reverse cowgirl to the missionary position and then finally to doggy style. His strokes were long and steady as he penetrated her from different angles until he found her G-spot.

"Yyyyeeeeeessssss!" she cried with pleasure. "Harder! Harder! Yes, tear that shit up."

Yetta felt like she was having an out-of-body sexual experience. If she died right now, she would die happy. Her clit was on fire, and she began to frantically rub it with her fingers, stimulating herself even more. Sensing the urgency in her moans, he pumped harder and stronger, penetrating her even deeper.

It seemed like they both climaxed in unison. Yetta's body jerked with the force of her tenth orgasm of the night. Moments later, and physically drained, her lover slumped down on her, never pulling out. They lay on the floor savoring the feeling. Eventually they shifted around until Yetta found a comfortable spot in his arms and fell asleep.

~ ~ ~

The next morning, she woke up all alone. She looked around but he was nowhere to be found, and he had left her a note:

Sorry I had to leave so early, but had to go tie up some loose ends. I'll hit you later when we can meet up again, 'cause I need some more of that good good.

You know who!

Yetta smiled at the thought of knowing that she rocked his world. She got off the floor trying to get herself together so she could get back home before her brother had a heart attack. She quickly got in the shower with a million thoughts running through her mind.

She hoped that the double-cross game she was playing didn't come back and bite her in the ass like it did with her father. There were so many reasons she resented her brother that she couldn't begin to name them. What she did know was that she blamed him for the death of their parents. That was how he rose up the chain to supremacy. Now she wanted to be the one sitting on the thrown. That's why she set it up for the cartel to go to war with the Organization.

"Soon I'll be the queen of the North, and everybody will bow down to me," she said to herself.

TWELVE

"Mmmmmm!"

The nurse looked up from the sponge bath she was giving Supreme. She was washing his genitals and thought she heard something. She stood up and looked out of the room to make sure no one was there. Whenever she had to bathe Supreme, she would secretly use that time to play with his manhood, hoping that she would get a quick arousal out of him.

When she didn't see anyone, she went back over to continue doing her job. She sat next to him, then started fondling his dick again, this time without the sponge. As she rubbed his dick with one hand, she slipped her other hand under her uniform, inside her panties. It easily slipped right into her already wet pussy. She closed her eyes imagining that it was

Supreme's dick. As she continued stroking her pussy and massaging his penis, she felt it starting to stiffen up.

"Mmmmmm!"

This time when she opened her eyes, Supreme was staring at her, and his mans was at full attention. The nurse jumped up off the bed.

"I'm so sorry, sir, please don't fire me," she begged.

"Calm down, ma," he said in a groggy voice. "Where am I?"

"You're at the Chavez Estate. Your brother brought you here to keep you safe. I am the nurse that has been attending to you for the last few months."

"Where is my brother? I need to speak with him now," he demanded.

"I'll get him for you right away, sir," she said, leaving the room. She was terrified that he was going to turn her in, so she walked down the hallway on pins and needles.

Supreme tried to sit up, but his body was in so much pain that he could barely move. He looked around at the luxurious room he was in, and had to muster up a smile knowing his brother had to have picked it for him. A couple minutes later, Justice came rushing into the room. He ran straight to his twin brother and gave him a hug, not realizing that he was hurting him.

"Ouch, Bro!"

"My bad, Bro. I'm just glad to see you up. How are you feeling?"

"I'm hurting all over. Damn, I should have been wearing a vest like you always told me," Supreme replied, feeling over all the bandages that covered his bullet wounds.

"Don't worry, we're gonna get all those motherfuckers back," Justice stated. "All I want you to do is get some rest."

"It was those crooked-ass cops that shot me," Preme snapped.

"We know, Bro. As we speak, my team is paying them a visit."

~ ~ ~

"Sit your ass on that bench and don't move," the officer said, pushing the drug dealer down.

"Don't put your fucking hands on me again. You're lucky these cuffs are on me, or else we would be having a different conversation."

"Oh really! So you're a tuff guy now, huh? Let's see how tuff you really are then," he stated, walking back toward him.

"What the hell is going on over there?" the desk sergeant asked.

"Nothing, Serg," the officer replied. "He's just pissed off that he was caught red handed selling dope on the street."

"You two, get him booked and processed," the

sergeant said, ordering the officers to take him away. "You go get started with the paperwork."

"Yes, sir!" Then he turned to the drug dealer. "Don't let me catch you again," the officer smirked, walking away.

"Suck my dick, cracker," the young boy replied as they escorted him away to the holding cell.

For some reason the police station had been empty all day. There were only two prisoners in the holding cell on 65th and Woodland. There was one male and one female in their tank. The shift was just changing when about ten men dressed in all black pulled up on the corner in two utility vans and marched into the precinct carrying assault rifles. They had on full body armor, and from the look on their faces, they weren't there to talk.

"What the hell is going on . . ." was all the desk sergeant said before all hell broke loose.

Bullets were flying in every direction, hitting

anything that wasn't wearing black. The men didn't even bother to wear masks because they knew they weren't leaving anyone breathing. People were ducking behind desks, trying to get out of the way but the shooters stormed through the place like they were trained in the military. One officer was calling for backup when a fleet of bullets sent him straight to the afterlife.

"Get to the armory and make sure no one is able to get the weapons," the lead shooter yelled out to his men.

Just like that, three of them peeled off from the formation and headed toward the armory. They took out all the cameras on their way. They couldn't risk the eye in the sky seeing them, even though they knew they were on a suicide mission. Four cops had made it inside and were loading up sub-machine guns when the men stormed the room.

"Look out!" one of the officers shouted, but it

was too late. All four were ripped to shreds by the barrage of bullets.

"Set the explosives and let's go."

The team planted the bomb and set the timer, then rushed back toward the front of the building. As they passed the holding cell area, the young bull that just came through yelled out to them.

"Yo, get me out of here."

"You want out?" the man said, stopping in front of the cell.

"Yeah, get me the fuck out of here, man. Hurry up!"

"No problem, I got you," he said. Without hesitation, he shot the young bull three times in the face. "Now you're free, lil nigga."

When they made it back to the front, there were bodies sprawled out all over the place, including five of their own. This was one of the worst, if not the worst, massacre in Philly. They made it out the door just as the explosives went off. It wasn't enough to bring the building down, but, however, it did do some eternal damage. As soon as the men went to pull off, what looked like a hundred cops surrounded their vehicles. The shooters had no place to go, and they knew it.

"This is the police. Get out of the vehicle with your hands in the air," the captain yelled into the bullhorn. "You are surrounded. This is your only warning to comply."

Regular uniform officers from every borough were on the scene, blocking off a three-block radius, trying to keep pedestrians and innocent bystanders safe. Knowing they had nowhere to go, the leader signaled to his team that it was showtime. As if they knew what each other was thinking, they opened the doors to the van and let their guns do the talking for them.

Cops were dropping like flies as the men in black

moved in sync as one. They were under fire too, but due to their armor, the bullets were bouncing off of them. Snipers were positioned on the roof and started picking them off one by one with head shots. Once the leader saw his last four men go down, he hit a button causing one of the vans to go up in flames, killing more police officers. He tried to make a run for it, but was met by Agent Pryor.

"Federal agent, don't move!"

"I will never let you lock me inside some fucking cage."

As soon as he went to raise his weapon, the agent shot him at point blank range in the head. He dropped his weapon and died before he hit the ground. Once the carnage was over, besides the ten gunmen dying, over fifty cops were dead, and counting. Federal agents arrived on the scene in full force to investigate the bloodbath that the men caused. Little did they know, it wasn't over yet.

~ ~ ~

At the federal building on Market Street, they had just received a call stating that a bomb was inside. They sounded the alarm, evacuating the building, and all the employees rushed out waiting for the bomb squad to arrive and clear it. While everyone stood around conversing about different subjects, a fleet of SUVs circled the block a few times unnoticed, then suddenly stopped right in the middle of the street.

The men jumped out carrying AK-47s and just started firing at anything moving. Downtown became a scene from a movie as innocent people became casualties of war. Agent Roman was getting out of his car when the shooting started. He quickly jumped on the radio requesting backup.

"Ten thirteen, ten thirteen! Federal building is under attack, agents need assistance. I repeat, agents need assistance," he said then hopped out to help his friends.

Agent Pryor heard the 10-13 over the radio and immediately jumped in her car, followed by a dozen other agents, and headed to help their comrades. She already knew what was going on, and just hoped that they would get there before it looked like the scene at the police station.

Agent Roman rushed through the crowd of running people, with his weapon aimed in the ready position. As soon as he saw his targets, he let it go with no hesitation.

BOCA! BOCA! BOCA! BOCA! BOCA! BOCA! BOCA!

His shots found their targets, taking out three of the gunmen. As he went to aim his weapon at another gunman, someone leaned up from their hiding spot and fired.

BOC! BOC!

The shots hit him dead in the chest, knocking him

off his feet. Before he could recuperate, the shooter ran up on him.

"What is this about?" Agent Roman struggled to get out, holding his chest.

"Wrong place, right time," the gunman stated with a smirk.

The gunman aimed his gun and let off three more rounds, hitting the agent twice in the chest and once in the forehead. The agent never had a chance to even get a round off. He died in the middle of Market Street. The rest of the gunmen continued shooting until they ran out of bullets. When the shooting stopped, all the ones that were left standing hopped back in the SUVs and fled the scene.

Agent Pryor arrived to yet another horrific crime scene. This one was so bad that the sight of it made her lose everything she ate that morning. She spilled her guts out all over the street.

"Are you okay, ma'am?" one of the agents asked.

"Hell no I'm not okay. Look at this shit. We were played from the beginning, and now this is the outcome," she said, looking around. "No, I'm fucking pissed off right now. I want to kill the motherfuckers that are behind this shit."

Everyone was scrambling around in search of survivors. Agent Pryor needed to find her partner and make sure he was alright. He was the one who placed the initial "officer in distress" call. She had been trying to make radio contact but was unsuccessful. She was checking everywhere, when one agent stopped dead in his tracks. He looked over to where Agent Pryor was placing a sheet over one of the victims.

"Ma'am, I think you should see this."

Agent Pryor walked over to where the other agent was standing, already fearing the worst. Her fears were confirmed when she found Agent Roman lying in a pool of his own blood. Tears began falling nonstop as she bent down and cradled him in her arms.

"Don't worry, I'm going to get this asshole. I promise," she said, not caring about all the blood that was soaking into her shirt.

THIRTEEN

Since awakening from his coma, Supreme had been trying to get his strength back. He was now able to walk around without the help of his trainer or a wheelchair. He was determined not to let his getting shot stop him from having his brother's back. They were separated twice already counting the lil stint he did in prison waiting to beat his case, and that wasn't going to happen again. Even though he hadn't seen his adopted sister in a while, Elizabeth made an effort to come see her brother. She stayed by his side, along with Kreasha, while he was in the coma. The only time she left was when she needed to. Her boyfriend broke up with her because she didn't show him any affection or attention. She was crushed but knew it must wasn't meant to be.

"Ugghhhh," Supreme screamed, finishing his last

set of leg presses. He was in his girl's mother's basement, finishing his last set before taking a shower.

"Good job," his physical trainer replied. She used to babysit him when they were younger, and now she had been putting him through hell for the last two months, trying to get him back to the strong man he used to be. "I won't be here tomorrow, but I will see you on Wednesday. Just don't overwork yourself okay?"

"I'll try not to, as long as my girl don't wear me out, if you know what I mean," Preme smirked.

"You are too much, Supreme," she laughed, heading upstairs. "I'll see you later."

"Be safe, Tara."

She waved bye to him and left. Supreme headed upstairs to take a shower, when he saw Kreasha's mom standing on a stool cleaning the ceiling fan. He stared at her ass for a moment, then looked away. She had on a pair of tight shorts that hardly covered her ass. He had forgotten how she always walked around the house like that, without a care in the world. It never affected him until now. Maybe it had something to do with him not being intimate in a while.

"Oh shit, you scared me," Kimberly said, holding her chest.

"My bad! I was just heading upstairs to take a shower. Do you need any help with that?" he asked, wiping his face with the towel.

"No, I'm almost done now."

"Okay, if you need me I'll be in my room," he stated, heading up the steps. When he got into his room, he undressed and got in the shower. The water was soothing on his body as he closed his eyes and relaxed. He had a flashback of that day he got pulled over, and then when the shooter tried to take his life. His eyes opened quickly, and his breathing was heavy. It calmed down once he realized where he was. "Damn, I'm tripping," he said to himself. He got dressed and took a drive to the shooting range on Spring Garden Street. He wanted to get back right, because he knew with the beef still going on, he was gonna have to be ready to lay something down. The accuracy was still there, and he was more than pleased with the results. He stayed for over three hours before going home. Supreme decided to FaceTime Kreasha to check up on her at school. She told him she would be coming back home in two days, after her midterms were over. He never liked the fact that she wanted to go off to college, but he understood. She wanted her law degree so she could practice law. Their dream had been to go together, but the streets had taken that away for now. Since she was on the path to success, Supreme made sure she didn't want for anything. That's why he had everything from the four cars to the two houses in her name. By the time they finished talking, it was almost midnight. She needed to get some rest so she would be ready. He went downstairs in the living room and sat by the fireplace, then turned on Netflix to watch the episodes of *Power* he had missed. About an hour into it, Kreasha's mom came downstairs. "I see somebody else couldn't sleep either, huh?" she asked, walking over and sitting next to him on the floor.

"Naw, I just wanted to catch up on my show. I haven't had the chance to see any of this season yet," he replied.

"Mind if I watch with you?"

"Not at all," Supreme said, standing up. "Do you want something to drink?"

"Sure, thank you!" she replied, getting comfortable on the floor next to the fire. She grabbed the throw blanket from the couch and put it over her, then took two pillows and placed them on the floor.

"Here you go! One Hypnotic for you, and my favorite E&J for me," Supreme stated, passing her the drink. He sat back down and leaned back on the pillow.

They watched two episodes of *Power* together before Preme nodded off. Kimberly adjusted the blanket so they could share it. She turned the television off and scooted down next to him. The amber hue from the fireplace provided the only light in the room and outlined the silhouette of his face. Kimberly lay there studying how handsome Supreme was. She now understood why her daughter was so attracted to him. She leaned in so close to him that she could smell the liquor on his breath. She slid a hand inside her sweatpants and could feel her pussy already getting wet.

Kimberly kissed Supreme on the lips, tasting the leftover E&J on them. Making sure he wasn't awake, she leaned in and gave him another kiss while sticking two fingers inside her. Supreme, thinking it was Kreasha, reached over and grabbed her ass cheeks. His hand moved up to her hips and pulled her close to him. Without even opening his eyes, he began pulling her sweats off.

He scooted down under the blanket, aligning his mouth with her womanhood, and without hesitation explored it. His warm, thick tongue opened her southern lips as he licked her gently. He circled her clit while french kissing her lips, and feasted on her soaking wet pussy.

"Ohh," she moaned as she massaged the back of his head while falling victim to his delicious head game. Her legs weakened as he bit down on her love box.

As he continued biting down on her, it drove her so crazy that she nearly lost her mind. All her life she had never had someone who paid so much attention to her needs as he was doing at this moment.

"What are you doing to me?" Kimberly whispered as she began to quiver in ecstasy.

Supreme inserted one, two, then three fingers inside her. Kimberly's body was so responsive to his touch that she started gyrating on his hand, squeezing her vaginal muscles around his fingers as he tickled her insides and palmed her clit. He curved his fingers, hitting her G-spot.

"Wait! Ooh no, wait, Preme, shit," she whined.

The pressure was building inside of her, and she felt as if she would pee on herself. It felt so good that she didn't want to stop it. Her pussy lips were so swollen that it looked as if he had beaten them up, and her clit throbbed for attention.

"Put your mouth on me, please, baby, right now," she moaned.

Preme's fingers worked her over as he simultaneously kissed her clit, and that was all she could take. Kimberly screamed as her liquids poured out of her. Supreme licked her gently as he eased up from under the blanket.

"What the fuck!" Supreme said, standing up when he realized that it wasn't Kreasha he had pleased, but her mother.

"Shhhh," Kimberly replied, pushing him down onto the couch then standing over him. "Just go with the flow, okay? You're backed up, I'm backed up. Let's just share this moment."

Before he was able to protest, she had his manhood in her hands, stroking it, tracing the veins that throbbed in his dick. She noticed how perfectly thick and long it was. Not able to hold back any longer, he pulled her down onto his lap, filling her walls. Kimberly worked her hips and released her muscles, allowing him total access to her body. His fingers dug into her hips as he lifted and then lowered her onto his dick. Their rhythm was slow and sensual as he pulled one of her tout nipples into his mouth, sucking on it.

Bolts of electric pleasure shot up her spine, and Kimberly picked up her pace, grinding into him with passion. Her nails were clawing into his back. Preme kissed her on the lips, and the feeling of his tongue dancing in her mouth sent him over the edge. His stroke quickened, and he went deeper and deeper, killing the pussy.

"Oh shit, ma," he bellowed, pumping faster until he spilled his seed deep inside her.

"Mmmmmm! Shit, that felt so fucking good," Kimberly replied, lying on him.

"This was a one-shot deal. We can't do this shit again, and your daughter can never find out about this," he stated.

Supreme lifted her up off of him and headed up to his room. He couldn't believe that he just laid pipe to his girl's mom. Even though it was good, he felt guilty about the whole situation. Once his head hit the pillow, all those thoughts quickly evaporated, and he was out for the count.

The next day, they acted as if nothing happened the night before. They both went their separate ways and did what normal people do. Supreme had to meet up with Justice to get shit popping together. There was about to be even more bloodshed, and this time he would be one of the ones pulling the trigger.

FOURTEEN

oosie Mandela, I am the people's choices. We can take it there, but I'll take it much farther. Dude you don't know me so you can't drink my bottle. Why when I was gone you ain't do nothing for my daughter? Paper-plate living, niggas hating cause I'm ballin. Borrowing his bitch, fucked up and spoiled her. You don't wanna see me, all I do is make a call. We have no specific victims, we want all y'all. Ride for the team, .45 with a beam. Plenty murder scenes. So I advise you not to fuck wit 'em . . . G-o-r-r-i-double-l-a. It's levels to this shit, like my nigga Meek say . . ."

Supreme and Justice rapped along with Boosie as they drove down 676, on their way to see a friend. Behind them was a fleet of SUVs, with four men in each. They were all armed with assault weapons.

"It's good to have you back by my side, Bro," Justice said, turning the music down.

"No doubt! It's good to be out of that fucking bed," he replied. "Yo, I have some crazy shit to tell you, Bro."

"What's up?"

"Why Ms. Kimberly seduce me last night?"

"Serious? Damn, her body is tight work. Was it good?"

"Man, that shit was banging, Bro. I want to hit that shit again, but I'm not fucking around, and she says something to Kreasha."

Justice listened to his brother rant on about last night, the whole time thinking about how his girl gave up the pussy easily. That's when a thought came to his mind.

"Yo, let's play the switch game on her. We never had the chance to do that when we were little, so let's catch up for old times."

"You're crazy, Bro," Supreme said.

"No, I'm serious. She will never know."

"We'll talk about that later, after we handle our business. It's game time," Supreme said as they parked a few houses away from the one they were looking for.

Two of the SUVs kept driving, and parked around the corner, while the third one parked at the top of the block.

"So what, we just walk up and knock on the door?" Supreme asked as they strolled up the block looking for the address on the piece of paper in his hand.

"Exactly!" Justice responded.

They finally found the house they were looking for and walked through the metal gate and up on the porch.

KNOCK! KNOCK! KNOCK!

~ ~ ~

"I told you that we wouldn't have enough evidence to prosecute that case. Now her lawyer will eat that shit up. Find me another witness that we can turn, and then come holla at me," District Attorney Edward Alston said into the Bluetooth.

He was on his way home after a hard day of work. The judge he hated most was trying to let a well-known drug dealer off the hook due to a technicality that was his investigator's fault. Now he only had a week to gather the evidence that he needed to proceed with the case. Edward pulled into the driveway and turned the engine off. He grabbed his briefcase out of the backseat, along with the Chinese food his wife asked him to pick up, then headed inside.

"Hey, I'm home. I have dinner with me," Ed said, sitting the food down on the dining room table.

When he didn't get a response, he set his briefcase down and walked toward the living room, where he heard the television on. As he looked in the room, he noticed his wife and kids sitting on the couch looking nervous.

"What the fuck is wrong with you? Why are you looking at me like that? I know you heard me calling you."

"Come on in and join the party," Justice said, aiming his gun in Ed's direction.

You could see the scared look on his face once he saw the two men with guns in hand, holding his family hostage. He was worried more about his family's safety than his own. Edward walked over toward where his family was sitting, with his hands half in the air, hoping that these assailants just wanted to rob him and leave.

"If it's money you want, I'll give it to you," Ed told them.

"What makes you think we want your money? Naw, this is bigger than that, my nigga. You are

SUPREME & JUSTICE 3

gonna set something up for us, and you might make it out of this unscathed."

"You come in here threatening my family with guns, then tell me that I have to help you set something up? How dare you—"

CRACK!

The sound of the weapon smashing over his head caused his oldest daughter to scream out for her father. He grabbed his face as blood escaped the left side of his face.

"Daddy!" she screamed, reaching out for him.

"If you don't want your children to become bastards, I suggest you do what he says," Supreme said with a smile on his face.

"Please, Edward, just give them what they want so they can leave."

"Yeah, Edward, listen to your bitch," Justice shot back.

Not wanting his kids to be traumatized for the

rest of their lives, Ed had no other choice but to comply with their demands. He wished that he had his gun on him, but it was in the safe in his bedroom. Supreme and Justice ran down the plan and told him that he better follow it down to the T.

~ ~ ~

Deputy Mayor Alston, Director McMillan, and a couple other members of the Organization, all sat in the conference room waiting for the person who called the meeting to enter. Edward walked in the room looking nervous, followed by a woman holding a tray of drinks. She passed everyone a glass before heading back out.

Ed sat in silence, stroking the hair on his face as he looked around the room at the other members. Catrena sat across from him, studying his expression. Knowing her brother all her life, she could tell something was bothering him. She just couldn't figure it out. Whatever it was, she knew it was serious, but even her wildest imagination couldn't prepare her for what she would soon witness.

"So what's so damn important that you drag us out at this time of night?" Director McMillan asked, taking a sip of his drink.

"Yeah, what's going on, Ed?" Catrena chimed in.

"And where are the rest of the members? They should all be here."

"We'll fill them in later. Now what's up?" Captain Harris said, impatiently waiting.

Ed didn't comment at first. He just stared at everyone sipping on their drinks. Finally he stood up, remembering what he was here to do. He cleared his throat then spoke with words that were carefully chosen.

"I brought you all here to let you know that we will be moving forward with our initial plans to sweep the areas from 29th and Diamond, to the Johnson Holmes projects. There will be no more drug running in those areas. I've already filed for the warrants, and the judge is scheduled to sign off on them first thing in the morning. I've assembled a group taskforce combining DEA, ATF, and local law enforcement to handle this. Federal as well as state will assist in prosecuting these bastards and putting them behind bars for a very long time."

"Then we can put our product back on the street?" McMillan asked.

"Exactly! We will control everything, with no outside interference," Ed replied.

This made everyone happy knowing that money was about to be flowing once again. They all smiled and gave Ed a nod of approval. The Organization had just conquered yet another obstacle that had tried to push them out and failed.

"Is there something else?" Catrena asked, sensing there was more.

"No," he lied. He knew that if he said something,

his family was dead. "Let's toast to the resurgence of the Organization."

"I'll drink to that," McMillan replied as they held their drinks up.

Once they set their glasses down, that's when shit took a turn for the worst. Each one of them started feeling dizzy.

"What the hell is wrong with me?" Captain Harris asked, holding his head, trying to shake it off.

"I'm sorry, they made me do it," Ed stated nervously.

"You motherfucker," Director McMillan snapped, reaching for his weapon. He tried to raise it but didn't have the strength. It fell out of his hand, onto the floor.

They all started choking and falling to the floor. The door suddenly kicked open, and in came everyone's worst nightmare. Supreme, Justice, and Dom stood there ice grilling the members of the

Organization. Their weapons were down by their sides.

"Looks like the gang's all here, except for the mayor and his crew," Justice said. "I hope you all enjoyed your drinks because they may be your last." The drinks they had a few minutes ago were laced.

"Fuck the formalities," Supreme blurted out. "I want to know who tried to body me. Somebody needs to start talking right fucking now."

No one said anything, so Supreme decided to help them hurry up and make up their minds. He stood over Captain Harris and put two rounds in the back of his head.

BOOM! BOOM!

Blood spattered all over the people lying next to him. Supreme then walked over to the female that was trying to crawl away, and kicked her in the face as hard as she could. She fell on her face, knocking her front teeth out of their socket. Supreme pulled out a hunting knife, then rammed it through her neck. He twisted it, then yanked it out. She died right there as the blood shot out of her neck like a garden hose.

"I think somebody needs to answer my brother's question," Dom spoke up. This was the first time she had actually ridden out with both twins without Worlds. Usually she would be side by side with her man. "Answer him, nigga!"

"Whatever you're gonna do, go right ahead. We're not telling you shit," the director moaned in so much pain.

"Okay, have it your way. Kill them all," Justice said, aiming his weapon at the remaining group of people.

"Wait, wait, I'll tell you what you want, just don't kill me please," Ed yelled, hoping to save his and his sister's life.

"You have ten seconds," Supreme told him.

Edward started spilling his guts without even a

second thought. The Organization looked at him with fire in their eyes. Even though Catrena knew why he was doing it, she still called him a rat in her head. When they heard the name, Dominique and Justice both looked at each other in disbelief. Now they realized how their whole operation was targeted and how everything they put in work for was under scrutiny. Supreme's eyes turned black, and his heart cold.

"Thanks for the info. Here's your cheese, you rat," Justice said.

Without hesitating, he shot Ed three times in the chest. Dom and Preme followed suit, and they killed everybody in the building. When they walked out, Supreme motioned to his gang of killers to handle the rest of Ed's family. He had no remorse for the order he just gave. They lived by the code of the streets: no witnesses. They hopped in their vehicle and fled before anyone saw them.

The taking over of Diamond Street and Johnson Holmes projects was all Justice's idea. That was one of their biggest goldmines, so when the Organization thought they were about to have control of those blocks, they were excited. Too bad for them, it was all a dream. They easily fell for the bait, and because of it, they lost their lives.

"Handle that," Supreme said into his cellphone. After he ended the call, he turned to Justice. "I think it's time to pay a visit to an old friend."

"I was thinking the same thing," Justice replied with the look of a stone-cold killer.

FIFTEEN

"Here they come," Leneek whispered as she gripped her .45 handgun and pressed her back against the wall.

"Shut the fuck up!" Whoopie whispered back. He pulled the ski mask over his face.

They had been waiting at the house for their guests for over two hours, anticipating their return. It wasn't hard to locate these creeps because they were the flossing type. Leneek had been trying to get at them for a minute now, and finally picked the right time to handle shit. Whoopie held the riot pump and pointed it toward the door as he casually stood in front of the sofa.

When the people walked in the door and turned on the light switch, they found themselves looking down the barrel of the riot pump. They froze in their tracks.

"Welcome home," Whoopie said, walking toward them.

The man's friend never even noticed Leneek creeping up behind them until she stuck her pistol to his neck.

"Fuck!" he said, putting his hands behind his head. He already knew the drill. "You can take off the mask, Whoopie. It ain't no secret who you are."

He kept shaking his head, regretting not being more cautious. If only he had paid attention, he wouldn't be suffering the consequences.

"You're right." Whoopie snatched his mask off and looked into the man's eyes.

The man also knew that it was only a matter of time before Justice was going to send his team after them. Leneek removed her mask also and just stood there. There was a brief moment of silence before Leneek finally spoke.

"Y'all know what we came for, so fuck the small talk. Take us to the stash." She pressed her gun into the man's back.

"I don't keep the money here," the man replied, shrugging his shoulders. "There's nothing in the house."

Leneek smiled and looked at Whoopie, who had his gun on the other man. She gave him a nod, and the sound of the pump erupted, putting a giant size hole through his chest.

"What the fuck!" the man yelled in shock as he watched his man's guts fly all over the floor and his body drop right beside him.

"Don't lie to me again," Leneek said in a calm voice. "We've been watching you bring money up in this motherfucker for a couple of weeks now. You have a week's worth of trap money in here, and I want it. Don't worry, Justice ain't the one who sent us either. Now, I'ma ask you one more time, and if you lie, I'm a let my boo do his thing. Do we understand each other now?"

The man glanced at Whoopie, who had an insane glare in his eye, and he knew that look all too well. He'd seen Whoopie put work in plenty of times, and knew he wasn't afraid to lay a nigga down.

"My trigger finger is itching, and I'm ready to pop off," he smirked.

"Damn!" the man yelled. "It's underneath the floor in a safe."

Leneek laughed, and nodded at Whoopie again. He aimed the pump at the man's leg and let off another round, nearly severing his leg from his body. The man screamed out in a lot of pain.

"Why are you playing with your life, nigga? We already checked the fucking safe. That is where you keep this, right?" she said, pulling out the 9mm from the back of her waist. "I know you didn't think we were rookies? You watch too many fucking movies if you thought I was gonna let you open that safe and start blasting. This is the last warning you're gonna get from me. Where is the cash at?"

"It's in the freezer in the basement."

"In the freezer? I would have never thought to look there." Leneek smiled, knowing she was about to come up.

Whoopie watched the guy while Leneek rushed down the steps and headed to the deep freezer. She cracked open the freezer, moved around some frozen vegetables, and found zip lock bag after zip lock bag of neatly stacked hundred-dollar bills.

"This is what I'm talking about," she said to herself. She grabbed a couple of trash bags and loaded all the money in them, then headed back up the stairs.

Leneek walked back in the room with a smile on her face, letting Whoopie know that the money was where he said it was. She gave him a head nod, signaling him to handle his business so they could get the fuck out of there. Whoopie was like Leneek's puppet; whatever she said do, he would do it. Almost instantly, he blew the man's head off his body, rocking him to sleep forever. He would definitely be having a closed casket at his funeral. That's if they could even verify they body.

Blood leaked from his body, turning the beige carpet maroon. The air began to stink of human waste. The man had eased his bowels on himself because of his relaxed muscles. Whoopie stared at the body, smiling. The smell had become so familiar, it didn't even bother him anymore. He stepped over the body like it was a piece of litter on a city street, and followed Leneek down the stairs, where they both gathered up the trash bags and dragged them back upstairs. They threw the bags in the trunk and sped off with a lil over a half million dollars.

~ ~ ~

ERNEST MORRIS

"That's the spot right there. Nigga, you better not bust yet! Keep hitting that spot, daddy," Leneek moaned as she gripped the kitchen seat tightly. She had nothing on but a pair of high heels and a smile.

Whoopie had his pants dropped around his ankles, one foot out, and his Timberlands on as he grinded slowly in circles, trying to hit every wall inside of Leneek. His balls swung back and forth with every stroke, hitting her clitoris every time, and it was driving her crazy.

"I got you, ma."

Whoopie gripped Leneek's ass cheeks and massaged them as he went to work on her. His sweat, along with Leneek's juices, hit the ceramic floor, and the sounds of sex echoed throughout the kitchen. Whoopie had a habit of keeping his boots on when he had sexual intercourse with Leneek. He knew they would provide more grip, and that meant better sex.

Leneek felt Whoopie's warm dick pulsate so hard

170

inside of her, it felt like his soldier had its own heartbeat.

"Oh my goodness!" She gripped the sink even tighter as he gave her the businesses. She began playing with her pussy, feeling her orgasm about to approach.

Whoopie knew what was about to come, so he sped up, and the sound alone drove both of them crazy. Leneek's knees buckled as she climaxed and exploded, staining his boots. She almost lost her balance, and held the sink to keep herself up as her legs quivered uncontrollably. Whoopie pulled out in time to release himself on her lower back.

"Damn, you make me love you even more every time," Leneek said, out of breath, hovering over the sink.

"I love you too, baby. I'm sorry, but I had to handle that. It's something about robbing a nigga for a half mill that drives me crazy."

"No apologies needed. That shit makes my pussy wet every time also. You handled your shit though." Leneek put her hand up for a high five.

"I hate to spoil y'all's little moment, but your services are needed elsewhere," a voice said. They both turned toward the sound and were staring down the barrel of two cannons. "Damn, your body is tight."

Leneek realized she wasn't wearing any clothes, and tried to cover herself. Whoopie wanted to reach for his burner sitting on the counter, but thought twice about it.

"I wouldn't try that if I was you. I'll put your brains all over that fucking counter," Footie replied, finger twitching around the trigger.

"What is this about, and who sent you?" Leneek asked, not caring anymore if they stared at her naked body.

"That's on a need-to-know basis, and right now

you don't need to know," Cash answered. Tired of going back and forth, he yanked the tablecloth from the table and tossed it to Leneek. "Put that on. We have to go."

"My clothes are sitting on the chair. I'm not putting on no fucking tablecloth," Leneek replied with an attitude.

"Bitch, if I say wear that shit, you will wear it," Footie said, getting in her face.

"Motherfucker, get away from her," Whoopie said as if he was about to intervene. Cash smacked him across the face with the butt of the gun, ending any fight he thought he had in him.

"Okay, okay! Chill out," Leneek yelled, seeing Whoopie's face covered in blood.

Seeing that they now realized who was in charge, Cash motioned for Footie to grab Leneek's clothes off the chair, while he kept his weapon aimed at them. Once she was dressed, they tied them both up and gagged their mouths. They placed them inside the SUV and headed to their destination. This meeting was long overdue, and nothing would be the same afterward.

SIXTEEN

Justice scanned the parking lot as he sat in a black F-150 pickup truck. He tried his best to act like he fit in with the other people sitting in their cars. He glanced at the clock and sucked his teeth.

"Where this nigga at?" Justice said to himself.

There were five kilos of dope in the bag next to him for the buyer he was waiting on for the last thirty minutes. They had been doing business for quite some time now, and he was never this late before. That kind of bothered Justice.

"That's why I don't like fucking coming down this bitch," he mumbled.

He was just about ready to leave, when he saw his man pulling up in a candy-apple-red Lexus. He hated when he came to do business in a flashy car. As Moe parked the car, Justice peeped his surroundings. He grabbed the bag and stepped out of the car, and headed over to Moe's vehicle. He opened the door, and the loud music was blasting from the speakers. Moe quickly turned the volume down. He extended his hand for a shake.

"What's up, Just? Sorry I'm running so late. Traffic was crazy."

"Man, you got the cash? 'Cause I need to get back home. I have shit to do," Justice said, thinking about his brother. Supreme told him to go handle his business while he attended to some other shit.

"Man, what's wrong with you today? You're not your usual self, bro," Moe asked, sensing his impatience.

"Nothing," Justice replied. He kept looking around making sure everything was on the up and up with his man. "So where's the cash?"

Moe reached in the backseat for the book bag and set it on his lap. He opened it up to show him that it was all there.

"I got you all together right here, bro. You have my product?"

Justice and Moe exchanged bags, looking at the contents inside. Moe could tell that this batch was purer than the last package. He looked at Justice and gave him a head nod.

"I'm out," Moe told him.

"Yeah, I'm out of here too," Justice replied.

He opened the door and was about to get out, when something just didn't sit right with him. He closed the door, and in one swift motion pulled out his burner, aiming it at Moe.

"What's up, bro?"

"Shhhhhh," Justice motioned for him to shut up, by placing his finger over his lips.

He reached over and patted Moe's chest. Just as he suspected, Moe was wearing a wire. Justice ripped his shirt open, grabbed the wire, then tossed it out the window. He knew he only had a few minutes before whoever was on the other end of that wire would be there trying to save Moe. The only good thing was, Moe never mentioned his name.

"Why did you turn into a fucking snitch, huh? After all I did for you, this is how you repay me, nigga?" Justice snapped.

"They had me on some gun charges, bro, I'm sorry."

"Nigga, I'm not trying to hear that shit you talking. What you can do is take that sad-ass excuse with you, 'cause your time is up, my nigga."

BOOM! BOOM!

The sound from his cannon rang out like thunder, hitting Moe in the chest. He slumped over on the steering wheel. Justice grabbed the bag of work from off the backseat and stepped out the car. At that moment, he didn't care who saw what just happened. He jumped in his car and took off as people gathered around Moe's car in shock, watching the dead body bleed out over the seat and his clothes.

Knowing he couldn't go back home right now,

Justice jumped on the highway, heading toward Maryland to hide out for a while. He called his brother to give him a heads up on what was going on. Supreme informed him that he would tie up some loose ends real quick and hit the road himself. When he hung up with his brother, he told Kreasha that she was going to have to run the operation until they were able to return back home. The heat was on, now that his brother had killed a federal witness. They would be searching for the both of them now.

"When will you be back?" Kreasha asked.

"I'm not sure, but call me from a throwaway phone only, okay?" Supreme said, giving her a kiss on the cheek. "I have to go see someone before I go, but make sure you don't take shit from anybody okay? You are the boss, and they work for you."

"Okay, baby," she replied a bit sadly.

She was kind of pissed because he had just come back into her life after being in a coma. Now he had to go into hiding for a while because of his brother.

She was getting tired of Justice ruining their lives because they were twins, but knew that Justice didn't trust anyone else, not even Ray. She still felt guilty for fucking him, and tried blaming it on the fact that they were identical and she couldn't tell them apart. In all actuality, she was torn between the two and didn't know what to do.

Now that she was running shit now, she had to put on her big-girl panties and act accordingly. It didn't matter that her man was feared all over town; nobody feared her. Plus they were leaving her in the middle of a war with the Organization. To her the Organization were criminals hiding behind badges and political power. Supreme made sure that Ray provided her with all the security she needed. He also let two of their most trusted killers know to be on standby just in case. Kreasha watched as her man left to join his brother.

SEVENTEEN

*L*eneek and Whoopie were both chained to a metal pipe in an abandoned building on Westminster Street. Both of their mouths were gagged, and their clothes had been cut off, leaving them naked. It didn't help that it was cold outside, so they both shivered where they stood. Leneek was wondering what this was all about, because she had no clue. Footie walked in staring at Leneek, shaking his head.

"Mmmmm," she said, trying to get his attention.

"My bad, were you trying to say something?" Footie asked, removing the gag.

"Why are we here?"

"You'll find that out in a few minutes, sexy," he replied, squeezing her breast. All Whoopie could do was watch with rage in his eyes. "Oh, you want to hurt me now for doing this!" He slipped a finger into her pussy, causing her to squirm a little.

"Don't put your fucking hands on me again," she said, ice grilling him.

"What the fuck you gonna do, bitch?" Footie blurted out. Just when he was about to continue, the basement door opened.

They all looked in the direction of the door and waited to see who was coming. Cash walked through the door first, followed by Supreme toting a .357 snub nose with a silencer attached. He had a very serious look on his face, and Whoopie could tell he was about to suffer for some shit Leneek had done, once again. Supreme cleared his throat then spoke with words that were carefully chosen.

"I sat and thought long and hard before I came down here," he stated in a little over a whisper. All eyes were focused on him, and there was no other sound in the room besides his voice. Supreme looked from one face to the other, while Cash and Footie stood by his side, also with their weapons drawn. "The last thing a man ever wants to do is wonder about the loyalty of his team. Leneek, I'll start with you. You are the reason our trap houses were hit, right? Before you lie, think about it."

"I didn't have anything to do with that, Preme. You trusted me with your life, and I would never do anything to jeopardize that," she pleaded.

"That's what I'm talking about, Neek. You were one of the few people I did trust with everything I had. There were only a couple of people that knew where the main houses were, and for some strange fucking reason, they were the ones hit. I lost a lot of good soldiers in the process too."

"Come on, Preme. She didn't have anything to do with that. She knows how you get down when it comes to snakes," Whoopie stated, now that his gag was off.

"See, I'm glad you're speaking up for your bitch, because the one that double-crossed me is also the same person that was behind me getting hit up. Nobody expected me to survive that kind of hit, but I did." He paused and looked in the faces of Leneek and Whoopie. He had to admit that they were tight lipped and rocking with each other. "I'm gonna give one of you the chance to own up to what you've done, and make amends with your higher power. If you sit here and play dumb, I'm gonna do you real dirty. Now which one of you tried to murk me?"

"We had nothing to do with it," Whoopie replied.

"Supreme, it wasn't us," Leneek chimed in.

"Y'all gonna continue to play this shit all the way out, huh? I gave you the chance to tell me the truth, but that time has passed by."

Supreme nodded to Cash, and he ran up the stairs. When he came back down he was followed by another set of footsteps. Both Leneek and Whoopie's eyes looked like they were gonna pop out of their sockets. Neither one was expecting to see the person staring back at them.

"Point out the motherfucker that you said been working with the Organization," Supreme said with clenched teeth. He gripped the .357 tightly in his hand.

Whoopie saw the look in Supreme's eyes. It was the same look Justice had shown so many times before, and murder would be the only solution to restore his sanity.

"It was me," Whoopie blurted out. "I'm the one that tried to kill you. I found out that she was in love with you and Justice, and I resented you for it. I'm sorry, man."

"No, it was actually both of you," the stranger said, finally speaking up. "You wanted his territory and knew that in order for that to happen, you needed to get rid of your biggest threat, so you made a deal with the Organization."

"That motherfucker is lying to you. She had nothing to do with it," Whoopie replied.

"I'm a part of the Organization, so I know everything that's going on. You and this bitch bit off more than you could chew. Now suffer the consequences. Did you know that you were already going to die?"

"Please don't do this to us," he begged.

"Just shut up and stop acting like a bitch," Leneek said, tired of his whining. She looked at Preme without an ounce of remorse. "Do what you gotta do, nigga, I'm not scared of you. Go to hell, pussy."

"You first!" Preme said, walking right up to her and aiming at her head.

Pssst! Pssst!

The bullets went straight through her head and came out the other end. Her head popped backward, then leaned forward. Her body twitched momentarily before sitting still for good. Cash walked over and put two more bullets in her heart to make sure. Whoopie pissed on himself as he cried like a bitch.

"Shut that nigga up and call the cleanup crew to take care of the bodies," Preme said, walking over and shaking the stranger's hand. "I have to go, but hit me up when you have something else for me. This is for you."

Supreme passed the stranger a fat envelope full of cash for the info that was provided. They walked out of the basement and hopped in their separate cars. Supreme needed to get out of dodge before the feds spotted him. He had rented a car for him and Kreasha, just in case they were watching any of theirs. Once he was in the car, he took out his cellphone and made a call.

"I have a small concern."

"What's that, my friend?" the person on the other end asked.

"See, I was just thinking to myself, if it was so easy for you to turn on the Organization, how do I know that you won't also turn on me? Who's to say that you're not playing both sides like my former associates were?"

"I don't know, you just have to trust me."

"See, that's where your wrong. I don't have to do shit, and I don't trust anyone except my brother," he replied.

"Where is all this coming from? We were just together minutes ago, and everything was good. I thought we had an agreement."

"That's not important right now. However, my friend, what is important is that I don't leave any loose ends."

"So what are you saying?" the person replied, looking around and checking the rearview mirror.

"Your services are no longer needed," Supreme said, ending the call.

He dialed another series of numbers and pressed send. He didn't even have to be around to know what the outcome was. While they were in the basement, a bomb was planted inside the car, and all Preme had to do was enter the code to detonate it. The next call he made was to Kreasha, and after talking with her and knowing she had everything under control, he jumped on the highway and headed for Maryland.

EIGHTEEN

*I*t had been four months since Supreme and Justice left the business to be run by Kreasha, and she had been making great progress. The Organization found out about the death of their second in charge, and for some reason instead of them retaliating, they backed off altogether. The streets had too many bodies dropping far as police and criminals were concerned. The city of Philadelphia was in an uproar, so the governor was about to declare a state of emergency and have the National Guard dispersed. That meant that the city would be under martial law. Mayor Street couldn't have that, so he told what was left of the Organization to lay low and get rid of anything that had something to do with it.

Ray's cousin Jose had taken over for him and was the one doing business with Kreasha. Ray needed to return to Mexico to take care of the family business since his father was on his deathbed. Kreasha would pick the product up, then take it to the chemist to cook, cut, and bag it up. She had eight girls that took four-man shifts, bagging and packing the dope. Like Supreme and Justice, her only stipulation was that they only wore panties while working, which they all agreed to since they were benefitting from it substantially.

Lately the product hadn't been the same. The potency of it diminished tremendously, and she thought that it was her chemist skimming from the top. She instantly had him killed to make a statement that nobody steals from her. When the next shipment arrived, she hired another chemist to cook the dope and got the same result. Kreasha was going to call Preme and confide in him but didn't want him to think that she couldn't handle it. So she decided to take care of it herself.

When she called Ray from a secured line, he

assured her that the product had not been tainted in any way. The black tar came from Africa and the dope was 100 percent pure, so something was wrong.

"Let me get back to you when I find out what's wrong," Ray told her.

"Make sure you do that," Kreasha replied, ending the call.

She already knew what was going on because she had someone test the product. Instead of it being cut with fentanyl, it was being cut with baby powder. She called Jose to confront him about the situation. He told her to meet him in Atlantic City, because he didn't want to talk on the phone about anything. When she drove out there to the pier he requested, Kreasha spotted the most beautiful yacht she had ever seen, and standing there waiting was Jose. She was very impressed by the whole thing.

"Hola hermosa agradable en verte otra vez," Jose said in Spanish trying to flirt with her.

"What I tell you about that? Speak English to

me," she replied.

"My bad, ma. I said, 'Hey, beautiful, nice to see you again.'"

"Oh, okay! Anyway, I came to find out what's going on with the product. It's been tampered with, and that's not a good look."

"Why don't you have a drink with me?" he said, pouring two glasses.

Kreasha took the glass from him and sipped on it. He explained to her that they had given her a couple of bad batches and that everything would be back to normal with the next shipment. They talked for hours while drinking and enjoying the view. She didn't know if it was the liquor or the fact that she hadn't been intimate with her man in so long, but she was really horny right now.

"I need to use the bathroom real quick."

"It's right down the hall to the right," Jose said.

When she stepped inside, she sat on the edge of the toilet and pulled out her toy that she kept inside her purse for special occasions. She pulled down her shorts and panties enough to have access to her pussy, then turned on the vibrator and inserted it into her wetness. With her eyes closed, she let it do its job until the battery died. Kreasha was pissed as she fixed her clothes and headed back up to the deck with Jose.

"Is everything okay?" he asked.

"Yeah!" Kreasha replied, sitting down in the chair. She was still turned on, and disappointed that she didn't relieve herself.

It didn't help that Jose was standing there with no shirt on and his abs were on full display. The sweat on his chest had the sun glistening off of him. She had to cross her legs to stop her juices from trying to escape. He knew what she was doing in the bathroom because he heard the sound of the vibrator when he walked past. He decided to play off of it.

"Listen, since you're here, would you like to go for a swim with me?"

"I didn't bring a bathing suit," Kreasha replied.

"Look inside that cabinet. There are brand new ones on the shelf. I'll meet you in the pool," he said, stripping down to a pair of Speedos.

Kreasha's mouth watered at the print coming from his shorts. She knew she needed to get out of there before she did something stupid.

"I'm going to have to pass on that invitation. I need to get home," she said, turning her head and standing up.

Jose walked over and gave her a hug. The hug lasted too long, and she could feel his dick poking at her pelvis.

"Just let me eat your pussy. I won't say anything if you don't," he whispered in her ear. "I heard the vibrator when you were in the bathroom, and I know it's hard, your man being gone for so long."

As much as Kreasha wanted to pull away, she didn't. It'd been a while since she had been touched by a man. She was tired of toys and needed that feeling badly.

"I'm not fucking you, just so you know," she moaned.

Even though she knew she would regret it, she submitted her body. He removed her shorts and panties, then lifted her onto the counter. For the next twenty minutes Jose ate her pussy so good, that she came multiple times. She was ready to give him some pussy until she received a call from Supreme. She stopped and grabbed her stuff, then left before things really got out of control.

"What the hell did I just do?" Kreasha said to herself as she jumped on the New Jersey Turnpike, heading back to Philly.

All kinds of thoughts ran freely through her mind. The biggest one of them all was if Supreme found out about all of her indiscretions, she was done. Kreasha talked to him and told him about the shipments. She informed him that she was handling it, and not to worry about anything. Hopefully it was under control, or her ass was cooked.

~ ~ ~

A week later she received the same product, and when she contacted Ray about it, he told her that he wasn't trying to hear that shit and she needed to have his money. He said that his product was as pure as it comes. She called Jose and he said the same thing. Kreasha was so stressed out that she passed out on her way to her car. When she woke up and looked around, she was sitting in a hospital bed. The doctor walked in to talk to her and informed her that she was sixteen weeks pregnant.

"Are you serious?"

"Yes, ma'am, I assure you that the test is correct," she told Kreasha.

"I'm just shocked."

"I understand your concern. That's why I'm going to schedule you for a follow-up, and I would like to put you on prenatal care."

"Thank you," Kreasha replied.

The doctor discharged her, and as she rode home in a cab, she couldn't believe that she was knocked up, because she was on birth control. She needed to call and let Supreme know what was going on, but she wanted to tell him in person. She hoped that once she delivered the news, he would come back with her.

When she called him and told him that it was very important that she speak with him, he told her to tell him what was going on. Kreasha was persistent that she speak to him in person, and he told her to come on down there. She hurried home and packed an overnight bag, checked all the locks on the door, then hopped in the car.

NINETEEN

After driving three hours on the highway, Kreasha entered the city of Maryland, for a meeting she requested with Preme. She wasn't too happy about driving down there to tell him the news, but if this meant being able to see her man, she didn't mind. Since Preme had left her in charge of the business because the feds were onto him, she really had the chance to learn just what he had to deal with. Kreasha was hoping that this would bring them back together from being so distant.

She allowed her GPS to guide her to the seafood restaurant where Preme was supposed to be waiting for her. When she arrived, the smell coming from the Atlantic Ocean began bringing back memories of her and Jose's little meeting that had taken place just a week ago. It wasn't necessarily what transpired that gave her this thought, but more or less the yacht that she had fallen in love with. She wanted one for herself.

When Kreasha entered the restaurant, she was led to a table where she found Preme having his way with a bushel of crabs. Seeing him made her feel guilty, but she would never tell him what she did when she visited Jose. After being seated, she looked over at him, and he was staring at her, not looking too happy. She thought he knew what was going on.

"Supreme, listen. I know what you're gonna say . . ."

"Kreasha, please," he interrupted her. "Don't speak for me. Now, what was so important that you had to travel way out here to talk?"

"I had to talk to Jose and . . ."

"Stop, stop, stop," he cut her off again. "Kreasha, you know what?" He took a second to wipe his hands and mouth off before continuing. "So I guess you still having a problem with the product was a lie, huh?"

SUPREME & JUSTICE 3

"No, it wasn't! If you would just listen and let me speak . . ." She paused to get his attention.

"What the fuck does this have to do with you and Jose? I thought I told you that you're the boss?"

"I understand, but that mutherfucker is watering down the product that I'm supposed to be selling. If you don't fix it, his family will have to identify his retarded ass at the morgue. I'm putting my life and your name on this shit, and getting garbage in return. Fix this shit, Supreme, or I will."

Supreme could sense the seriousness in her voice, but it was her eyes and body language that let him know that it was more than just business that she came down here to discuss.

"I'm sensing something else going on. What's really up with you?" Preme asked, staring into her eyes, trying to figure out her in game.

"I came here because I missed you. This long-distance shit is getting fucking old, Preme. I need you home with me. I'm tired of using fucking toys to

201

satisfy my needs. I don't need this stress right now. I'm pregnant, sexually frustrated, and in need of some fucking dick in my life," she said, feeling her panties getting wet at the sight of her man.

"Wait a minute, you're what?" Supreme asked, not believing what he was hearing.

"I'm pregnant, baby," she repeated with a smile. "Now since I'm here, can I spend the night with my baby daddy?"

"Come on, let's get out of here and go somewhere, where we can be alone," Supreme said, grabbing her by the hand and leading her out of the restaurant. Kreasha missed her fiancé and was more than happy to go back to his hotel room.

After she was finished with him, it was back to business. Kreasha planned on running the business despite her pregnancy, but she wasn't going to do it by herself. She needed her man with her even if she had to sacrifice his brother in the process. She was the queen of the streets, and he was her king, even if he was laying low for a while. It was her time to make everyone feel her presence, and after she made love to her man, that's exactly what she intended on doing.

"I can't wait to have you inside of me," she whispered into his ear as they drove to his hotel.

"I guess that makes two of us," Supreme replied, reaching over between her legs and rubbing her pussy through her jeans.

Kreasha opened her legs to give him better access, and reciprocated the favor by sticking her hand in his shorts, rubbing his erection. By the time they arrived at Supreme's room, they both were ready to explode.

~ ~ ~

When Kreasha returned to Philly, she wanted to go pay Jose a visit. Since he wanted to have a meeting when she came back to discuss the product, she told herself that there was no time like the present. Since she was in the area, Kreasha decided to pick up her money from one of the stash spots on her way. When she turned on the block, Jose was standing outside of her crib with a couple of friends.

Kreasha got pissed because he was trying to sell dope that he had cut from her shit, and had the audacity to do it on her streets. That was the straw that broke the camel's back. She pulled up alongside them, then rolled down her window.

"Jose, let me speak with you for a minute," she said, waiting for him to come over to her vehicle.

"What's up, Kreasha?" he said like nothing was wrong. "I just wanted to see how this shit was moving since you said it was garbage."

"That shit is garbage. That's why I will be dealing with Ray directly, or not at all," she replied, giving him a blank expression.

"What the fuck are you saying, puta?" José said.

"I'm telling you that your services are no longer needed out here."

BOOM! BOOM! BOOM!

The sound of her .40 cal. was the only thing that could be heard, besides his friends gasping for air as if they had lost their breath. José's whole face was blown off. He died before he hit the ground. The mouths of the two dudes that were standing outside with him dropped wide open as they stood there in horror. Neither one of them could move. Kreasha then turned and aimed the cannon at them.

"Any questions?" They shook their heads no.

"Good!" she said, pulling off like nothing had just happened. She had just made a statement to the streets and also covered up a secret at the same damn time. What she really didn't know was, José's demise was the beginning of another war.

Text Good2Go at 31996 to receive new release updates via text message.

To order books, please fill out the order form below:
To order films please go to www.good2gofilms.com

Name:_____

Address:_____

City: _____ State: _____ Zip Code: _____

Phone:_____

Email:_____

Method of Payment: Check   VISA   MASTERCARD

Credit Card#:_____

Name as it appears on card: _____

Signature: _____

Item Name	Price	Qty	Amount
48 Hours to Die – Silk White	$14.99		
A Hustler's Dream - Ernest Morris	$14.99		
A Hustler's Dream 2 - Ernest Morris	$14.99		
Bloody Mayhem Down South	$14.99		
Business Is Business – Silk White	$14.99		
Business Is Business 2 – Silk White	$14.99		
Business Is Business 3 – Silk White	$14.99		
Childhood Sweethearts – Jacob Spears	$14.99		
Childhood Sweethearts 2 – Jacob Spears	$14.99		
Childhood Sweethearts 3 - Jacob Spears	$14.99		
Childhood Sweethearts 4 - Jacob Spears	$14.99		
Connected To The Plug – Dwan Marquis Williams	$14.99		
Connected To The Plug 2 – Dwan Marquis Williams	$14.99		
Deadly Reunion – Ernest Morris	$14.99		
Flipping Numbers – Ernest Morris	$14.99		
Flipping Numbers 2 – Ernest Morris	$14.99		
He Loves Me, He Loves You Not - Mychea	$14.99		
He Loves Me, He Loves You Not 2 - Mychea	$14.99		
He Loves Me, He Loves You Not 3 - Mychea	$14.99		
He Loves Me, He Loves You Not 4 – Mychea	$14.99		
He Loves Me, He Loves You Not 5 – Mychea	$14.99		
Lord of My Land – Jay Morrison	$14.99		
Lost and Turned Out – Ernest Morris	$14.99		
Married To Da Streets – Silk White	$14.99		
M.E.R.C. - Make Every Rep Count Health and Fitness	$14.99		
Money Make Me Cum – Ernest Morris	$14.99		
My Besties – Asia Hill	$14.99		

My Besties 2 – Asia Hill	$14.99		
My Besties 3 – Asia Hill	$14.99		
My Besties 4 – Asia Hill	$14.99		
My Boyfriend's Wife - Mychea	$14.99		
My Boyfriend's Wife 2 – Mychea	$14.99		
My Brothers Envy – J. L. Rose	$14.99		
My Brothers Envy 2 – J. L. Rose	$14.99		
Naughty Housewives – Ernest Morris	$14.99		
Naughty Housewives 2 – Ernest Morris	$14.99		
Naughty Housewives 3 – Ernest Morris	$14.99		
Naughty Housewives 4 – Ernest Morris	$14.99		
Never Be The Same – Silk White	$14.99		
Stranded – Silk White	$14.99		
Slumped – Jason Brent	$14.99		
Supreme & Justice – Ernest Morris	$14.99		
Supreme & Justice 2 – Ernest Morris	$14.99		
Supreme & Justice 3 – Ernest Morris	$14.99		
Tears of a Hustler - Silk White	$14.99		
Tears of a Hustler 2 - Silk White	$14.99		
Tears of a Hustler 3 - Silk White	$14.99		
Tears of a Hustler 4- Silk White	$14.99		
Tears of a Hustler 5 – Silk White	$14.99		
Tears of a Hustler 6 – Silk White	$14.99		
The Panty Ripper - Reality Way	$14.99		
The Panty Ripper 3 – Reality Way	$14.99		
The Solution – Jay Morrison	$14.99		
The Teflon Queen – Silk White	$14.99		
The Teflon Queen 2 – Silk White	$14.99		
The Teflon Queen 3 – Silk White	$14.99		
The Teflon Queen 4 – Silk White	$14.99		
The Teflon Queen 5 – Silk White	$14.99		
The Teflon Queen 6 - Silk White	$14.99		
The Vacation – Silk White	$14.99		
Tied To A Boss - J.L. Rose	$14.99		

Tied To A Boss 2 - J.L. Rose	$14.99		
Tied To A Boss 3 - J.L. Rose	$14.99		
Tied To A Boss 4 - J.L. Rose	$14.99		
Tied To A Boss 5 - J.L. Rose	$14.99		
Time Is Money - Silk White	$14.99		
Two Mask One Heart – Jacob Spears and Trayvon Jackson	$14.99		
Two Mask One Heart 2 – Jacob Spears and Trayvon Jackson	$14.99		
Two Mask One Heart 3 – Jacob Spears and Trayvon Jackson	$14.99		
Wrong Place Wrong Time – Silk White	$14.99		
Young Goonz – Reality Way	$14.99		
Subtotal:			
Tax:			
Shipping (Free) U.S. Media Mail:			
Total:			

Make Checks Payable To:
Good2Go Publishing
7311 W Glass Lane,
Laveen, AZ 85339

NOV 2017

CPSIA information can be obtained
at www.ICGtesting.com
Printed in the USA
LVOW07s1545111017
552035LV00011B/702/P